Tales of Two Countries

Maxim Gorky

Tales of Two Countries

Copyright © 2023 Bibliotech Press
All rights reserved

The present edition is a reproduction of previous publication of this classic work. Minor typographical errors may have been corrected without note; however, for an authentic reading experience the spelling, punctuation, and capitalization have been retained from the original text.

ISBN: 979-8-88830-113-5

CONTENTS

ITALIAN TALES

MAN AND THE SIMPLON

A blue lake is deeply set in mountains capped with eternal snow. A dark network of gardens descends in gorgeous folds to the water. White houses that look like lumps of sugar peer down from the bank into the lake; and everything around is as quiet and peaceful as the sleep of a child.

It is morning. A perfume of flowers is wafted gently from the mountains. The sun is new risen and the dew still glistens on the leaves of trees and the petals of flowers. A road like a grey ribbon thrusts into the quiet mountain gorge—a stone-paved road which yet looks as soft as velvet, so that one almost has a desire to stroke it.

Near a pile of stones sits a workman, like some dark coloured beetle; on his breast is a medal; his face is serious, bold, but kindly.

Placing his sunburnt hands on his knees and looking up into the face of a passer-by who has stopped in the shade of a chestnut-tree, he says:

"This is the Simplon, signor, and this is a medal for working in the Simplon tunnel,"

And lowering his eyes to his breast he smiles fondly at the bright piece of metal.

"Oh, every kind of work is hard for a time, until you get used to it, and then it grows upon you and becomes easy. Ay, but it was hard work though!"

1

He shook his head a little, smiling at the sun; then suddenly he checked and waved his hand; his black eyes glistened.

"I was afraid at times. The earth must have some feeling, don't you think? When we had burrowed to a great depth, when we had made this wound in the mountain, she received us rudely enough. She breathed a hot breath on us that made the heart stop beating, made the head dizzy and the bones to ache. Many experienced this. Then the mother earth showered stones upon her children, poured hot water over us; ay, there was fear in it, signor! Sometimes, in the torchlight, the water became red and my father told me that we had wounded the earth and that she would drown us, would burn us all up with her blood—'you will live to see it!' It was all fancy, like enough, but when one hears such words deep in the bowels of the earth—in the damp and suffocating darkness, amid the plaintive splashing of water and the grinding of iron against stone—one forgets for the moment how much is fantasy. For everything was fantastic there, dear signor: we men were so puny, while the mountain, into whose belly we were boring, reached up to the sky. One must see in order to understand it. It is necessary to see the black gaping mouth cut by us, tiny people, who entered it at sunset—and how sadly the sun looks after those who desert him and go into the bowels of the earth! It is necessary to see our machines and the grim face of the mountain, and to hear the dark rumblings in it and the blasts, like the wild laughter of a madman."

He looked at his hands, set right the medal on his blue blouse and sighed.

"Man knows how to work!" he continued, with manifest pride. "Oh, signor, a puny man, when he wills to work, is an invincible force! And, believe me: in the end, the little man will do everything he wants to do. My father did not believe it at first.

"'To cut through a mountain from country to country,' he said, 'is contrary to the will of God, who separated countries by mountain walls; you will see that the Madonna will not be with us!' He was wrong, the old man; the Madonna is on the side of everyone who loves her. Afterwards my father began to think as I now think and avow to you, because he felt that he was greater and stronger than the mountain; but there was a time when, on holidays, sitting at a table before a bottle of wine, he would declare to me and others:

"'Children of God'—that was his favourite saying, for he was a kind and good man—'children of God, you must not struggle with the earth like that; she will be revenged on you for her wounds, and will remain unconquerable! You will see: when we bore into the mountain as far as the heart, when we touch the heart, it will burn us up, it will hurl fire upon us, because the earth's heart is fiery— everybody knows that! To cultivate the soil means to help it to give birth—we are bidden to do that; but now we are spoiling its physiognomy, its form. Behold! The farther we dig into the mountain the hotter the air becomes and the harder it is to breathe.'"

The man laughed quietly and curled the ends of his moustache with both hands.

"Not he alone thought like that, and he was right; the farther we went in the tunnel, the hotter it became, and men fell prostrate and were overcome. Water gushed forth faster from the hot springs, whole seams fell down, and two of our fellows from Lugano went mad. At night in the barracks many of us talked in delirium, groaned and jumped up from our beds in terror.

"'Am I not right?' said my father, with fear in his eyes and coughing more and more, and more and more huskily—he did, signor. 'Am I not right?' he said. 'She is unconquerable, the earth.'

"At last the old man lay down for the last time. He was very strong, my old one; for more than three weeks he struggled bravely with death, as a man who knows his worth, and never complained.

"'My work is finished, Paolo,' he said to me once in the night. 'Take care of yourself and return home; let the Madonna guide you!'

"Then he was silent for a long time; he covered up his face, and was nigh to choking."

The man stood up, looked at the mountains and stretched himself with such force that his sinews cracked.

"He took me by the hand, drew me to himself and said—it's the solemn truth, signor—

"'Do you know, Paolo, my son, in spite of all, I think it will be done: we and those who advance from the other side will meet in the mountain, we shall meet—do you believe that?'

"I did believe it, signor.

"'Well, my son, so you must: everything must be done with a firm belief in a happy ending and in God who helps good people by the prayers of the Madonna. I beg you, my son, if it does happen, if the men meet, come to my grave and say: "Father, it is done," so that I may know!'

"It was all right, dear signor, I promised him. He died five days after my words were spoken, and two days before his death he asked me to bury him at the spot where he had last worked in the tunnel. He prayed, but I think it was in delirium.

"We and the others who came from the opposite side met in the mountain thirteen weeks after my father's death—it was a mad day, signor! Oh, when we heard there, under the earth, in the darkness, the noise of other workmen, the noise of those who came to meet us under the earth—you understand, signor, under the tremendous weight of the earth which might have crushed us, puny little things, all at once had it but known how!

"For many days we heard these rumbling sounds, every day they became louder and louder, clearer and clearer, and we became possessed by the joyful madness of conquerors—we worked like demons, like persons without bodies, not feeling fatigue, not requiring direction—it was as good as a dance on a sunny day, upon my word of honour! We all became as good and kind to one another as children are. Oh, if you only knew how strong, how intensely passionate is one's desire to meet a human being in the dark, under the earth into which one has burrowed like a mole for many long months!"

His face flushed, he walked up close to the listener and, looking into the latter's face with deep kindling eyes, went on quietly and joyously:

"And when the last wall finally crumbled away, and in the opening appeared the red light of a torch and somebody's dark face covered with tears of joy, and then another face, and more torches and more faces—shouts of victory resounded, shouts of joy.... Oh, it was the best day of my life, and when I think of it I feel that I have not lived in vain! There was work, my work, holy work, signor, I tell you, yes!.... Yes, we kissed the conquered mountain, kissed the earth— that day the earth was specially near and dear to me, signor, and I fell in love with it as if it had been a woman!

"Of course I went to my father! Of course—although I don't know that the dead can hear—but I went: we must respect the wishes of those who toiled for us and who suffered no less than we do—must we not, signor?

"Yes, yes, I went to his grave, knocked with my foot against the ground and said, as he wished:

"'Father—it is done!' I said. 'The people have conquered. It is done, father!'"

AN UNWRITTEN SONATA

A young musician, his dark eyes fixed intently on far-off things, said quietly:

"I should like to set this down in terms of music":

Along a road leading to a large town walks a little boy. He walks and hastens not.

The town lies prostrate; the heavy mass of its buildings presses against the earth. And it groans, this town, and sends forth a murmurous sound. From afar it looks as if it had just burned out, for over it the blood-red flame of the sunset still lingers, and the crosses of its churches, its spires and vanes, seem red-hot.

The edges of the black clouds are also on fire, angular roofs of tall buildings stand out ominously against the red patches, window-panes like deep wounds glisten here and there. The stricken town, spent with woe, the scene of an incessant striving after happiness— is bleeding to death, and the warm blood sends up a reek of yellowish, suffocating smoke.

The boy walks on. The road, like a broad ribbon, cleaves a way amid fields invaded by the gathering twilight; straight it goes, piercing the side of the town like a rapier thrust by a powerful, unseen hand. The trees by the roadside resemble unlit torches; their large black heads are uplifted above the silent earth in motionless expectancy.

The sky is covered with clouds and no stars are to be seen; there are no shadows; the late evening is sad and still, and save for the slow, light steps of the boy no sound breaks the silence of the tired fields as they fall asleep in the dusk.

The boy walks on. And, noiselessly, the night follows him and envelops in its black mantle the distances from which he has emerged.

As the dusk grows deeper it hides in its embrace the red and white houses which sink submissively into the earth. It hides the gardens with their trees, and leaves them lonely, like orphans, on the hillsides. It hides the chimney-stacks.

Everything around becomes black, vanishes, blotted out by the darkness of the night; it is as if the little figure advancing slowly, stick in hand, along the road inspired some strange kind of fear.

He goes on, without speaking, without hastening, his eyes steadily fixed upon the town; he is alone, ridiculously small and insignificant, yet it seems as if he bore something indispensable to and long awaited by all in the town, where blue, yellow and red lights are being speedily lit to greet him.

The sun sinks completely. The crosses, the vanes and the spires melt and vanish, the town seems to subside, grow smaller, and to press ever more closely against the dumb earth.

Above the town, an opal cloud, weirdly coloured, flares and gradually grows larger; a phosphorescent, yellowish mist settles unevenly on the grey network of closely huddled houses. The town itself no longer seems to be consumed by fire and reeking in blood — the broken lines of the roofs and walls have the appearance now of something magical, fantastic, but yet of something incomplete, not properly finished, as if he who planned this great town for men had suddenly grown tired and fallen asleep, or had lost faith, and, casting everything aside in his disappointment, had gone away, or died.

But the town lives and is possessed by an anxious longing to see itself beautiful and upraised proudly before the sun. It murmurs in a fever of many-sided desire for happiness, it is excited by a passionate will to live. Slow waves of muffled sound issue into the dark silence of the surrounding fields, and the black bowl of the sky is gradually filled with a dull, languishing light.

The boy stops, with uplifted brows, and shakes his head; then he looks boldly ahead and, staggering, walks quickly on.

The night, following him, says in the soft, kind voice of a mother:

"It is time, my son, hasten! They are waiting."

"Of course it is impossible to write it down!" said the young musician with a thoughtful smile.

Then, after a moment's silence, he folded his hands, and added, wistfully, fondly, in a low voice:

"Purest Virgin Mary! what awaits him?"

SUN AND SEA

The sun melts in the blue midday sky, pouring hot, many-coloured rays on to the water and the earth. The sea slumbers and exhales an opal mist, the bluish water glistens like steel. A strong smell of brine is carried to the lonely shore.

The waves advance and splash lazily against a mass of grey stones; they roll slowly upon the beach and the pebbles make a jingling sound; they are gentle waves, as clear as glass, and there is no foam on them.

The mountain is enveloped in a violet haze of heat, the grey leaves of the olive-trees shine like old silver in the sun; in the gardens which cover the mountain-side the gold of lemons and oranges gleams in the dark velvet of the foliage; the red blossoms of pomegranate-trees smile brightly, and everywhere there are flowers.

How the sun loves the earth!

There are two fishermen on the stones. One is an old man, in a straw hat. He has a heavy-looking face, covered on cheeks and chin and upper lip with grey bristles; his eyes are embedded in fat, his nose is red, and his hands are sunburnt. He has cast his pliant fishing-rod far out into the sea, and he sits upon a rock, his hairy legs hanging over the green water. A wave washes up and bathes them, and from the dark toes clear, heavy drops of water fall back into the sea.

Behind the old man, leaning with one elbow on a rock, stands a tawny black-eyed fellow, thin and lank. On his head is a red cap, and a white jersey covers his muscular torso; his blue trousers are rolled up to the knee. He tugs with his right hand at his moustache and looks thoughtfully out to sea; in the distance black streaks of fishing boats are moving, and far beyond them, scarcely visible, is a white sail; the white sail is motionless, and seems to melt like a cloud in the sun.

"Is she a rich signora?" the old man inquires, in a husky voice, as he makes an unsuccessful effort to cross his knees.

The young man answered quietly:

"I think so. She has a brooch, and earrings with large stones as blue as the sea, and many rings, and a watch.... I think she is an American."

"And beautiful?"

"Oh yes! Very slender, it is true, but such eyes, just like flowers, and, do you know, a mouth so small, and slightly open."

"It is the mouth of an honest woman and of the kind that loves but once in her life."

"I think so too."

The old man drew in his rod, winked as he looked at the hook, and muttered with a laugh:

"A fish is no fool, to be sure."

"Who fishes at midday?" asked the youth, getting down on his knees.

"I," replied the old man, putting on fresh bait. And, having thrown the line far into the sea, he asked:

"You rowed her till the morning, you said?"

"The sun was rising when we got out on the shore," readily replied the young man, with a heavy sigh.

"Twenty lire?"

"Yes."

"She might have given more."

"She might have given much."

"What did you speak to her about?"

The youth seemed annoyed and lowered his head gloomily.

"She does not know more than ten words, so we were silent."

"True love," said the old man, looking back and showing his strong teeth in a broad smile, "strikes the heart like lightning, and is as dumb as lightning, you know."

The young man picked up a large stone and was about to throw it into the sea; but he threw it back over his shoulder, saying:

"Sometimes one cannot understand what people want with different languages."

"They say some day it will be different," said the old man, after a moments thought.

Over the blue surface of the sea, in the far-off milky mist, noiselessly glides a white steamer, like the shadow of a cloud.

"To Sicily," said the old man, nodding towards the steamer.

From somewhere or other he took a long, uneven, black cigar, broke it in two and, handing one half over his shoulder to the young man, asked:

"What did you think about as you sat with her?"

"Man always thinks of happiness."

"That's why he is always so stupid," the old man put in quietly.

They began to smoke. The blue smoke wreaths hung over the stones in the breathless air which was impregnated with the rich odour of fertile earth and gentle water.

"I sang to her and she smiled."

"Eh?"

"But you know that I sing badly."

"Yes, I know."

"Then I rested the oars and looked at her."

"Aha!"

"I looked, saying to myself: 'Here am I, young and strong, while you are languishing. Love me and make me happy.'"

"Was she feeling lonely?"

"Who that is not poor goes to a strange land if he feels merry?"

"Bravo!"

"I promise by the name of the Virgin Mary—I thought to myself—that I will be kind to you and that everybody shall be happy who lives near us."

"Well, well!" exclaimed the old man, throwing back his large head and bursting into loud bass laughter.

"I will always be true to you."

"H'm."

"Or—I thought—let us live together a little while; I will love you to your heart's content; then you can give me some money for a boat and rigging, and a piece of land; and I will return to my own dear country and will always, as long as I live, remember and think kindly of you."

"There's some sense in that."

"Then—towards the morning—it seemed to me that I needed

nothing, that I did not want money, only her, even if it were only for one night."

"That is simpler."

"Just for one single night."

"Well, well!" said the old man.

"It seems to me, Uncle Pietro, that a small happiness is always more honest."

The old man was silent. His thick, shaven lips were compressed; he looked intently into the green water. The young man sang quietly and sadly:

"Oh, sun!"

"Yes, yes," said the old man suddenly, shaking his head, "a small happiness is more honest, but a great happiness is better. Poor people are better-looking, but the rich are stronger. It is always so."

The waves rock and splash. Blue wreaths of smoke float, like nymphs, above the heads of the two men. The young man rises to his feet and sings quietly, his cigar stuck in a corner of his mouth. He leans his shoulder against the grey side of the rock, folds his arms across his chest, and looks out to sea with the eyes of a dreamer.

But the old man is motionless, his head has sunk on his breast and he seems to doze.

The violet shadows on the mountains grow deeper and softer.

"O sun!" sings the youth.

"The sun was born more beautiful,

More beautiful than thou!

Bathe me in thy light,

O sun!

Fill me with thy life!"

The green waves chuckle merrily.

LOVE OF LOVERS

At a small station between Rome and Genoa the guard opened the door of our compartment and, with the assistance of a dirty oiler, led, carried almost, a little, one-eyed, old man up the steps into our midst.

"Very old!" remarked both at the same time, smiling good-naturedly.

But the old man turned out to be very vigorous. After thanking his helpers with a pretty gesture of his wrinkled hand he politely and gaily lifted his shabby dust-stained hat from his grey head, and, looking sharply at the seats with his one eye, inquired:

"Will you permit me?"

He was given a seat at once. He then straightened his blue linen suit, heaved a sigh of relief and, putting his hands on his little, withered knees, smiled good-humouredly, disclosing a toothless mouth.

"Going far, uncle?" asked my companion.

"Only three stations!" he replied readily. "I am going to my grandson's wedding."

After a few minutes he became very talkative and, raising his voice above the noise made by the wheels of the train, told us as he swayed this way and that like a broken branch on a windy day:

"I am a Ligurian: we Ligurians are a strong people. I, for instance, have thirteen sons and four daughters; I confuse my grandchildren in counting them; this is the second one to get married—that's pretty good, don't you think?"

He looked proudly round the compartment with his lustreless but still merry eye; then he laughed quietly and said: "See how many people I have given to my country and to the king!"

"How did I lose my eye? Oh, that was long ago, when I was still a boy, but already helping my father. He was breaking stones in the vineyard; our soil is very hard, and needs a lot of attention: there are a great many stones. A stone flew from underneath my father's pick and hit me in the eye. I don't remember any pain, but at dinner my eye came out—it was terrible, signors! They put it back in its place and applied some warm bread, but the eye died!"

The old man rubbed his brown skinny cheek, and laughed again in a merry, good-humoured way.

"At that time there were not so many doctors, and people were much more stupid. What! you think they may have been kinder? Perhaps they were."

And now this dried-up, one-eyed, deeply wrinkled face, with its partial covering of greenish-grey, mouldy-looking hair, became knowing and triumphant.

"When one has lived as long as I one may talk confidently about men, isn't that so?"

He raised significantly a dark, crooked finger as though threatening someone.

"I will tell you, signors, something about people.

"When my father died—I was thirteen at the time—you see how small I am even now: but I was very skilful and could work without getting tired (that is all I inherited from my father)—our house and land were sold for debts. And so, with but one eye and two hands, I lived on, working wherever I could get work. It was hard, but youth is not afraid of work, is it?

"When I was nineteen I met a girl whom Fate had meant me to love; she was as poor as myself, though stronger and more robust; she, also, lived with her mother, an old woman in failing health, and worked when and where she could. She was not very comely, but kind and clever. And she had a fine voice—oh! she sang like a professional, and that in itself means riches, signors!

"'Shall we get married?' said I, after we had known each other for some time.

"'It would be funny, you one-eyed fellow!' she replied rather sadly. 'Neither you nor I have anything. What should we live on?'

"Upon my soul, neither I nor she had anything! But what does that signify to young love? You all know, signors, how little love requires; I was insistent and got my way.

"'Yes, perhaps you are right,' said Ida at last. 'If the Holy Mother helps you and me now when we live apart, it will be much easier for her to help us when we live together.'

"We decided upon it and went to the priest.

"'This is madness!' said the priest. 'Aren't there beggars enough in Liguria? Unhappy people, playthings of the devil, you must struggle against his snares or you will pay dearly for your weakness.'

"All the youths in the commune jeered at us, and all the old people shook their heads, I can tell you. But youth is obstinate and will have its way! The wedding day drew near; we were no better off than we had been before; we really did not know where we should sleep on our wedding night.

"'Let us go into the fields,' said Ida. 'Why won't that do? The Mother of God is equally kind to all, and love is everywhere equally passionate when people are young.'

"That is what we decided upon: that the earth should be our bed and the sky our coverlet!

"At this point another story begins, signors; please pay attention; this is the best story of my long life. Early in the morning of the day before our wedding the old man Giovanni, for whom I worked, said to me like this, his pipe between his teeth, as if he were speaking about trifles:

"'Ugo, you had better go and clean out the old sheep-shed and put some straw in it. Although it is dry there, and no sheep have been in it for over a year, it ought to be cleaned out properly if you want to live in it with Ida.'

"Thus we had a house!

"As I worked and sang, the carpenter Constanzio stood in the door and asked:

"'Are you going to live here with Ida? Where is your bed? You must come to me when you have finished and get one from me—I have one to spare.'

"As I went to his house Mary, the bad-tempered shopkeeper, shouted:

"'The wretched sillies get married and don't possess a sheet, or pillow, or anything else! You are quite crazy, you one-eyed fellow! Send your sweetheart to me.'

"And Ettore Viano, tortured by rheumatism and fever, shouted from the threshold of his house:

"'Ask him whether he has saved up much wine for the guests! Oh, good people, who could be more light-headed than these two?'"

In a deep wrinkle on the old man's cheek glistened a tear of happiness; he threw back his head and laughed noiselessly, pawing his old throat and the flabby skin of his face; his arms were as restless as a child's.

"Oh, signors, signors!" said he, laughing and catching his breath. "On our wedding morn we had everything that was wanted for a home—a statue of the Madonna, crockery, linen, furniture—everything, I swear! Ida wept and laughed, and so did I, and everybody laughed—it is not the thing to weep on one's wedding day, and they all laughed at us!

"Signors, words cannot tell how sweet it is to be able to say 'our' people. It is better still to feel that they are 'yours,' near and dear to you, your kindred, for whom your life is no joking matter, your happiness no plaything! And the wedding took place! It was a great day. The whole commune turned out to see us, and everybody came to our shed, which had become a rich house, as in a fairy-tale. We had everything: wine and fruit, meat and bread, and all ate and were merry. There is no greater happiness, signors, than to do good to others; believe me, there is nothing more beautiful or more joyful.

"And we had a priest. 'These people,' he said gravely, and in a manner suited to the occasion, 'have worked for you all, and now you have provided for them so that they may be happy on this the best day of their life. That is exactly what you should have done, for they have worked for you, and work is of more account than copper and silver coins; work is always greater than the payment that is given for it! Money disappears, but work remains. These people are happy and humble; their life has been hard but they have not grumbled; it may be harder yet and they will not murmur—and you will help them in an hour of need. Their hands are willing and their hearts as good as gold.' He said a lot of flattering things to me, to Ida and to the whole commune!"

The old man looked triumphantly, with his one eye, at his fellow-travellers, and there was something youthful and vigorous in his glance as he said:

"There you have something about people, signors. Curious, isn't it?"

It is spring-time, the sun shines brightly, and everyone is gay. Even the window-panes of the old stone houses seem to wear a cheerful smile.

Along the street of the little town streams a crowd in bright holiday attire. The whole population of the town is there: workers, soldiers, tradespeople, priests, officials, fishermen; all are intoxicated with the spirit of spring-time, talking, laughing, singing in joyous confusion, as if they were a single body overflowing with the zest of life.

The hats and parasols of the women make a medley of bright colours; red and blue balloons, like wonderful flowers, float from the hands of the children; and children, merry lords of the earth, laughing and rejoicing, are everywhere, like gems on the gorgeous cloak of a fairy prince.

The tender green leaves of the trees have not yet unfolded; they are sheathed in gorgeous buds, greedily drinking in the warm rays of the sun. Far off the sun smiles gently and seems to beckon us.

The impression seems to prevail that people have outlived their misfortunes, that yesterday was the last day of the hard shameful life that wearied them to death. To-day they have all awakened in high spirits, like schoolboys, with a strong, clear faith in themselves, in the invincibility of their will to overcome all obstacles, and now, all together, they march boldly into the future.

It was strange—strange and sad and suddenly depressing—to notice a sorrowful face in this lively crowd: it was that of a tall, strongly built man, not yet over thirty but already grey, who passed arm-in-arm with a young woman. He carried his hat in his hand, the hair on his shapely head glistened like silver, his thin but healthy face was calm and destined to remain for ever sad. The eyes, large and dark, and shaded by long lashes, were those of a man who cannot forget—who will never forget—the acute suffering through which he has passed.

"Notice that couple," said my companion to me, "especially the man: he has lived through one of those dramas which are enacted more and more frequently amongst the workers of Northern Italy."

And my companion went on:

That man is a socialist, the editor of a local Labour paper, a workman himself, a painter. He is one of those characters for whom science becomes a religion, and a religion that still more incites the thirst for knowledge. A keen and clever Anti-Clerical he was—just note what fierce looks the black priests send after him.

About five years ago he, a propagandist, met in one of his circles a girl who at once attracted his attention. Here women have learnt to believe silently and steadfastly; the priests have cultivated this ability in them for many centuries, and have achieved what they wished. Somebody rightly said that the Catholic Church has been built up on the breast of womankind. The cult of the Madonna is not only beautiful, as such heathen practices go, it is first of all a clever cult. The Madonna is simpler than Christ, she is nearer to one's heart, there are no contradictions in her, she does not threaten with Gehenna—she only loves, pities, forgives—it is easy for her to make a captive of a woman's heart for life.

But there he sees a girl who can speak, can inquire; and in all her questions he perceives, side by side with her naïve wonderment at his ideas, an undisguised lack of belief in him, and sometimes even fear and repulsion. The Italian propagandist has to speak a great deal about religion, to say incisive things about the Pope and the clergy; every time he spoke on that subject he saw contempt and hate for him in the eyes of the girl; if she asked about anything her words sounded unfriendly and her soft voice breathed poison. It was evident that she was acquainted with Catholic literature directed against socialism, and that in this circle her word had as much weight as his own.

Until latterly the attitude here towards women was far more vulgar and much coarser than in Russia, and the Italian women were themselves to blame for this; taking no interest in anything except the Church, they were for the most part strangers to the work of social advancement carried on by men and did not understand its meaning.

The man's self-love was wounded, the clever propagandist's fame suffered in the collisions with the girl; he got angry; lost his temper; occasionally he ridiculed her successfully, but she paid him back in his own coin, evoking his involuntary admiration, forcing him carefully to prepare the lectures he had to give to the circle she attended.

In addition to all this he noticed that every time he came to speak about the present shameful state of things, how man was being oppressed, his body and his soul mutilated—whenever he drew pictures of the life of the future when all will be both outwardly and inwardly free—he noticed that she was quite another being: she listened to his speeches, stifling the anger of a strong and clever woman who knows the weight of life's chains; listened to them with the rapt eagerness of a child that is told a fairy tale which is in harmony with its own magically complex soul.

This excited in him the anticipation of victory over a strong foe—a foe who could be a fine comrade, a valiant champion in the cause of a better future.

The rivalry between them lasted nearly a year, without calling forth any desire in them to join issue and fight their battle out; at length he made the first advance.

"Signorina is my constant opponent," he said, "does she not think that in the interests of the cause it would be better if we were to become more closely acquainted?"

She willingly fell in with his suggestion, and almost from the first word they entered upon a spirited contest: the girl fiercely defended the Church as the only place where the souls of the weary find rest, where before the face of the Madonna all are equal and equally pitiable, notwithstanding the differences in worldly seeming. He replied that it was not rest that people needed but struggle, that civic equality is impossible without equality in material things, and that behind the cloak of the Madonna is concealed a man to whom it is advantageous that people should remain miserable and unenlightened.

Thereafter these discussions filled their whole life, every meeting was a continuation of the one same endless, passionate theme, and every day the stubborn strength of their beliefs became more and more evident.

For him life was a struggle for the widening of knowledge, for the conquest of the forces of Nature, a struggle for the subjugation of mysterious energies to the will of man. It was meet that everybody should be equally armed for this struggle, which was to issue in Freedom and the triumph of Reason—the most powerful of all forces, and the only force in the world which acts consciously. For her life was a slow and painful sacrifice of man to the Unknown, the subjugation of Reason to that will the laws and aims of which are known to the priest only.

Nonplussed by this, he inquired:

"Why do you attend my lectures and what do you expect from socialism?"

"Yes, I know that I sin and contradict myself!" she confessed sorrowfully.

"But it is pleasant to listen to you and to dream about the possibility of happiness for all!"

Though not specially pretty she was slim and graceful, with an intelligent face, and large eyes, whose glance could be mild or angry, gentle or severe. She worked in a silk factory, lived with her old mother, her one-legged father and a younger sister who was attending a technical school. Sometimes she was happy, not boisterously, but quietly happy; she was fond of museums and old churches, grew enthusiastic over pictures and the beauty of which they were the token, and looking at them would say:

"How strange it is to think that these things have been hidden in private houses and that but one person had the right to enjoy them! Everybody must see the beautiful, for only then does it live!"

She often spoke in so strange a manner that it seemed to him that her words came from some dark crevice in her soul; they reminded him of the groans of a wounded man. He felt that this girl loved life and mankind with that deep mother love which is full of anxiety and compassion; he waited patiently till his faith should kindle her heart and this quiet love change to passion. The girl appeared to him to listen more attentively to his speeches and, in her heart, to be in agreement with him. And he spoke more passionately of the need for an incessant, active struggle for the emancipation of man, of the nation, of humanity as a whole, from the old chains, the rust of which had eaten into their souls, and was blighting and poisoning them.

Once, while accompanying her home, he told her that he loved her, and that he wanted her to be his wife. He was startled at the effect his words had on her: she reeled as though she had been struck, stared with wide-open eyes and turned pale; she leaned against the wall, and said, clasping her hands and looking, almost terrified, into his face:

"I was beginning to fear that that might be so; almost I felt it, because I loved you long ago. But, O God! what is going to happen now?"

"Days of your happiness and mine will begin, days of mutual work," he exclaimed.

"No," said the girl, her head drooping. "No; we should not have talked about love."

"Why?'

"Will you be married according to the laws of the Church?" she asked quietly.

"No!"

"Then, good-bye!"

And she walked quickly away from him.

He overtook her, tried to persuade her; she heard him out in silence and then said:

"I, my mother and my father are all believers, and will die believers. Marriage at the registrar's is no marriage for me; if children are born of such a marriage I know they will be unhappy. Love is consecrated only by marriage in a church, which alone can give happiness and peace."

It seemed to him that soon she would yield; he, of course, could not give in. They parted. As she bade him good-bye the girl said:

"Let us not torment each other, don't seek meetings with me. Oh, if only you would go away from here! I cannot, I am so poor."

"I will make no promises," he replied.

The struggle between two strong natures began: they met, of course, and even more often than before; they met because they loved each other, sought meetings in the hope that one or other of them would be unable to stand the torments of an ungratified longing which was becoming more and more intense. Their meetings were full of anguish and despair; after each one he felt quite worn out and exhausted; she, all in tears, went to confess to a priest. He knew this and it seemed to him that the black wall of people in tonsures became stronger, higher and more insurmountable every day, that it grew and parted them till death.

Once, on a holiday, while walking with her through a field outside the town, he said, not threateningly, but more as if to himself:

"Do you know, it seems to me sometimes that I could kill you."

She remained silent.

"Did you hear what I said?"

Looking at him affectionately she answered:

"Yes."

And he understood that she would rather die than give in to him. Before this "yes" he had embraced and kissed her sometimes; she struggled with him, but her resistance was becoming feebler, and he cherished the hope that some day she would yield, and that then her woman's instinct would help him to conquer. But now he understood that that would not be victory, but enslavement, and from that day on he ceased to appeal to the woman in her.

So he wandered with her in the dark circle of her life's horizon, lit all the beacons before her that he could; but she listened to him with the dreamy smile of the blind, saw nothing, believed him not.

Once she said:

"I understand sometimes that all you say is possible, but I think that is because I love you! I understand, but I do not believe, I cannot believe! As soon as you go away all that is of you goes away too."

This drama lasted nearly two years, and then the girl's health broke down: she became seriously ill. He gave up his employment, ceased to attend to the work of his organisation, got into debt. Avoiding his comrades, he spent his time wandering round her lodgings; or sat at her bedside, watching her wasting from disease and becoming more transparent every day, noting how the fire of fever glowed more and more brightly in her eyes.

"Speak to me of life, of the future," she asked him.

But he spoke of the present, enumerating vindictively everything that crushes us, all those things against which he was vowed to a lifelong struggle; he spoke of things that ought to be cast out of mens lives, as one discards soiled and worn-out rags.

She listened until the pain it gave her became unbearable; then touched his hand, and stopped him with an imploring look.

"I, am I dying?" she asked him once, many days after the doctor had told him that she was in a galloping consumption and that her condition was hopeless.

He bowed his head but did not answer.

"I know that I shall die soon," she said. "Give me your hand."

And, taking his outstretched hand, she pressed it to her burning lips and said:

"Forgive me, I have done you wrong. It was all a mistake—and I have worn you out. Now when I am struck down I see that my faith was only fear before what I could not understand, notwithstanding my desire and my efforts. It was fear, but it was in my blood, I was born with it. I have my own mind—or yours—but somebody else's heart; you are right, I understand it now, but my heart could not agree with you."

A few days later she died; he turned grey during her agony; he was only twenty-seven.

Not long ago he married the only friend of that girl, his pupil. It is they who go to the cemetery, to her—they go there every Sunday and place flowers on her grave.

He does not believe in his victory, he is convinced that when she said to him: "You are right," she lied to him in order to console him. His wife thinks the same; they both lovingly revere her memory. This sad episode of a good woman who perished gives them strength by filling them with a desire to avenge her; it gives their mutual work a strangely fascinating character, and renders them untiring in their efforts.

*

The river of gaily dressed people streams on in the sunshine; a merry noise accompanies its flow: children shout and laugh. Not everyone is gay and joyful; there are many hearts, no doubt, oppressed by dark sorrow, many minds tormented by contradictions; but we all go steadily forward. And "Freedom, Freedom is our goal!"

And the more vigour we put into it the faster we shall advance!

THE TRAITOR'S MOTHER

Many are the tales that may be told about mothers.

For several weeks now the town had been surrounded by a close ring of armed foes. Of nights bonfires were lit and a multitude of fiery red eyes looked out from the darkness upon the walls. They glowed ominously, these fires, as if warning the inhabitants of the town. And the thoughts they conjured up were of a gloomy kind.

From the walls it was apparent that the noose of foes was being drawn tighter and tighter. Black shadows could be seen moving this way and that about the fires. The neighing of well-fed horses could be heard, and the clatter of arms and the loud laughter and merry songs of men confident of victory—and what is more painful to listen to than the laughter and songs of the foe?

The enemy had filled with corpses the streams which supplied the town with water; they had burned down the vineyards around the town, trampled down the fields, and cut down the trees of the neighbourhood, leaving the town exposed on all sides; and almost every day missiles of iron and lead were poured into it by the guns and rifles of the foe.

Detachments of half-starved soldiers, tired out by skirmishes, passed along the narrow streets of the town; from the windows of the houses come the groans of wounded, the raving of men in delirium, the prayers of women and the crying of children. Everybody spoke quietly, in subdued tones, interrupting one another's speech in the middle of a word to listen intently to detect whether the foe was not commencing to storm the town.

Life became especially unbearable in the evening, when the groans and cries became louder and more noticeable in the stillness, when blue-black shadows crept from the far-off mountain gorges, hiding the enemy's camp and moving towards the half-shattered walls, and, over the black summits of the mountains, the moon appeared, like a lost shield battered by the blows of heavy swords.

Expecting no assistance from without, spent with toil and hunger, and losing hope more and more every day, the people looked fearfully at the moon, at the sharp crests and the black gorges of the mountains, at the noisy camp of the enemy—everything spoke to them of death and no single star twinkled solace to them.

They were afraid to light lamps in the houses; a thick fog enveloped the streets, and in this fog, like a fish at the bottom of a river, a woman flitted silently to and fro, wrapped from head to foot in a black mantle.

People, noticing her, asked one another:

"Is it she?"

"Yes!"

And they drew back into the recesses of the doorways or, lowering their heads, ran past her silently. The men in charge of the patrols warned her sternly:

"You are in the street again, Monna Marianna? Have a care! They may kill you and no one will trouble to search for the culprit."

She stood erect and waited, but the patrol passed her by, either hesitating or not wishing to harm her. Armed men walked round her as if she had been a corpse. Yet she lingered on in the darkness, moving slowly from street to street, solitary, silent and black, seeming the personification of the town's misfortunes. And around her, mournfully pursuing her, surged depressing sounds: groans, sobs, prayers, and the grim talk of soldiers who had lost all hope of victory.

She was a citizen and a mother, and her thoughts were of her son and of the town of her birth. And her son, a handsome but gay and heartless youth, was at the head of the men who were destroying the town. Not long ago she had looked at him with pride, as upon her precious gift to the fatherland, as upon a beneficent force created by her for the welfare of the town, her birthplace, and the place also where she had borne and brought up her son. Hundreds of indissoluble ties bound her heart to the ancient stones, out of which her ancestors had built the houses and the city walls; to the soil in which lay the bones of her kindred; to the legends, songs and hopes of her native people. And this heart now had lost him whom it had loved most and it was rent in twain; it was like a balance in which her love for her son was being weighed against her love for the town. And it was not possible yet to decide which love outweighed the other.

In this state of mind she walked the streets at night, and many, not recognising her, were frightened, thinking that the dark figure was the personification of Death which was so near to them all; those that recognised her stepped hurriedly out of her way to avoid the traitor's mother.

Once, in a deserted corner of the city wall, she came across another woman: she was kneeling by the side of a corpse, and praying with face uplifted to the stars; on the wall, above her head, sentinels were talking quietly; their guns clattered as they knocked against the projecting stones of the wall.

The traitor's mother inquired:

"Your husband?"

"No."

"Brother?"

"Son. My husband was killed thirteen days ago; this one to-day."

And, rising, the mother of the dead man said humbly:

"The Madonna sees everything, she knows everything, and I thank her!"

"What for?" asked Marianna, and the other replied:

"Now that he has fallen with honour, fighting for his fatherland, I can say that he sometimes caused me anxiety: he was reckless, fond of pleasure, and I feared lest for that reason he might betray the town, as Marianna's son has done, the enemy of God and men, the leader of our foes; accursed be he and accursed be the womb that bore him!"

Covering her face Marianna hurried away. The next day she went to the defenders of the town and said:

"Either kill me because my son has become your enemy, or open the gate for me, that I may go to him."

They replied:

"You are a citizen, and the town should be dear to you; your son is just as much your enemy as he is ours."

"I am his mother: I love him and deem it to be my fault that he is what he is."

Then they consulted together as to what should be done and came to this decision:

"We cannot, in honour, kill you for your son's sin; we know you could not have suggested this terrible sin to him; and we can guess how you must be suffering. You are not wanted by the town, even as a hostage; your son does not trouble himself about you; we think he has forgotten you, the fiend—and therein lies your punishment, if you think you have deserved it! To us it seems more terrible than death!"

"Yes," she said; "it is more terrible."

They opened the gate for her, and let her out of the town. For a long time they watched her from the wall as she made her way over this native soil, sodden now with blood shed by her son. She walked slowly, dragging her feet painfully through the mire, bowing her head before the corpses of the defenders of the town and repugnantly spurning the pieces of broken weapons that lay in her path—for mothers hate the instruments of destruction, believing only in that which preserves life.

She walked carefully, as though she carried under her cloak a bowl full of some liquid which she was afraid of spilling. And as she went on, as her figure grew smaller and smaller, it seemed to those who watched her from the wall that their former depression and hopelessness were disappearing with her.

They saw her stop when she had covered half the distance, and, throwing back her hood, gaze long at the town. Beyond, in the enemy's camp, they had also noticed her advancing alone through the deserted fields; figures, as black as herself, cautiously approached her. They went up to her, asked her who she was and whither she was going.

"Your leader is my son," she said, and none of the soldiers doubted her words. They walked by her side, speaking in terms of praise of the bravery and cleverness of their leader. She listened to them, her head raised proudly in the air and showing not the least surprise. That was just how her son should be!

And now she stands before the man whom she knew nine months before his birth; before him whom she had never put out of her heart. And he stands before her, in silk and velvet, and wearing a sword ornamented with precious stones. In everything fit and seemly, exactly as she had seen him many a time in her dreams—rich, famous and beloved!

"Mother!" he said, kissing her hands. "You come to me; it means that you have understood me, and to-morrow I will capture this accursed town!"

"In which you were born," she reminded him.

Intoxicated by his exploits, maddened by the desire for still greater glory, he spoke to her with the insolent pride of youth.

"I was born into the world and for the world, in order to strike it with astonishment! I spared this town for your sake—it is like a splinter in my foot and hinders me from advancing to fame as quickly as I could wish. But either to-day or tomorrow I will destroy the nest of these stubborn ones!"

"Where every stone knows you and remembers you as a child," she said.

"Stones are dumb; if men cannot make them speak let mountains speak of me—that is what I want!"

"But the people?" she asked.

"O yes, I remember them, mother. I need them also, for only in the memories of people are heroes immortal."

She replied:

"He is a hero who creates life, spiting death, who conquers death."

"No," he replied. "He who destroys becomes as famous as he who builds cities. For instance, we do not know whether Æneas or Romulus built Rome, but we know the name of Alaric and the other heroes who destroyed it."

"It has outlived all names," the mother suggested.

In this strain he spoke to her till sunset. She interrupted his vain talk less frequently and her proud head gradually drooped.

A mother creates, she preserves, and to talk about destruction in her presence is to speak against her understanding of life. But not knowing this the son was denying all that life meant for his mother.

A mother is always against death, and the hand that introduces death into people's dwellings is hateful and hostile to all mothers. But the son did not see it, blinded by the cold gleam of glory which kills the heart.

And he did not know that a mother can be just as resourceful, just as pitiless and fearless as an animal, when it concerns life which the mother herself creates and preserves.

She sat limply, with head bowed down. Through the open mouth of the rich tent of the leader could be seen the town where she had thrilled to the conception and travailed in the birth of this her firstborn child, whose only wish now was to destroy.

The purple rays of the sun bathed in blood the walls and towers of the town, the window-panes glistened ominously; the whole town seemed to be wounded, and from its hundreds of wounds streamed the red blood of life. Time went on, and the town grew black, like a corpse, and the stars like funeral candles were lit above it.

She saw with her mind's eye the dark houses where they were afraid to light the lamps, for fear of attracting the attention of the enemy; and the dark streets filled with the odour of corpses and the subdued whispers of people awaiting death—she saw everything and all; everything that was native and familiar to her stood out before her, awaiting her decision in silence, and she felt that she was the mother of all the people of her native town.

From the dark mountain-tops clouds descended into the valley, and like winged coursers sped upon the doomed town.

"Perhaps we shall make an attack to-night," said her son, "if the night is dark enough! It is not easy to kill when the sun looks into one's eyes and the glitter of the weapons blinds one—many blows are wasted then," said he, examining his sword.

"Come here," said his mother; "put your head on my breast; rest a while, and recall to your mind how happy and kind you were as a child, and how everybody loved you."

He obeyed, knelt against her and said, closing his eyes:

"I love only glory and you, because you bore me as I am."

"But women?" she asked, bending over him.

"There are many of them, one soon tires of them, as of everything sweet."

And finally she asked him:

"Do you not wish to have children?"

"Why? In order that they may be killed? Somebody like me would kill them; it would grieve me, and no doubt I should be too old then, and too weak, to avenge them."

"You are handsome, but as sterile as the lightning," she said, sighing.

He answered, smiling:

"Yes, as the lightning."

And he fell asleep on her breast like a child.

Then she covered him with her black cloak and plunged a knife into his heart. He shuddered, and died instantaneously, for she, his mother, knew well where her son's heart beat. And having pushed the corpse off her knees to the feet of the astonished guards, she said, pointing in the direction of the town:

"As a citizen I have done all I could for my fatherland: as a mother I remain with my son! It is too late for me to give birth to another, my life is of no use to anyone."

And the same knife, still warm with his blood—her blood—she plunged into her own bosom, and doubtless struck the heart. When one's heart aches it is easy to strike it without missing.

THE FREAK

It is a quiet sultry day, and life seems to have come to a standstill in the serene calm; the sky looks affably down at the earth, with a limpid eye of which the sun is the fiery iris.

The sea has been hammered smooth out of some blue metal, the coloured boats of the fishermen are as motionless as if they were soldered into the semicircle of the bay, which is as clear as the sky overhead. A seagull flies past, lazily flapping its wings; out of the water comes another bird, whiter yet and more beautiful than the one in the air.

In the distant mist floats, as if melting in the sun, a violet isle, a solitary rock in the sea, like a precious stone in the ring formed by the Neapolitan bay.

The rocky isle, with its rugged promontories sloping down to the sea, is covered with gorgeous clusters of the dark foliage of the vine, of orange, lemon and fig trees, and the dull silver of the tiny olive leaves. Out of this mass of green, which falls abruptly to the sea, red, white and golden flowers smile pleasantly, while the yellow and orange-coloured fruits remind one of the stars on a hot moonlight night, when the sky is dark and the air moist.

There is quiet in the sky, on the sea and in one's soul; one stops and listens to all the living things singing a wordless prayer to their God — the Sun.

Between the gardens winds a narrow path, and along it a tall woman in black descends slowly to the sea, stepping from stone to stone. Her dress has faded in the sun: brown spots and even patches can be seen on it from afar. Her head is bare; her grey hair glistens like silver, framing in crisp curls her high forehead, her temples and the tawny skin of her cheeks; it is of the kind that no combing could render smooth.

Her face is sharp, severe, once seen to be remembered for ever; there is something profoundly ancient in its withered aspect; and when one encounters the direct look of her dark eyes one involuntarily thinks of the burning wilderness of the East, of Deborah and Judith.

Her head is bent over some red garment which she is knitting; the steel of her hook glistens. A ball of wool is hidden somewhere in her dress, but the red thread appears to come from her bosom. The path is steep and treacherous, the pebbles fall and rattle as she steps, but this greyhaired woman descends as confidently as if her feet themselves could find the way. This tale is told of her in the village: She is a widow; her husband, a fisherman, soon after their wedding went out fishing and never returned, leaving her with a child under her heart.

When the child was born she hid it; she did not take her son out into the street and sunshine to show him off, as mothers are wont to do, but kept him in a dark corner of her hut, swaddling him in rags. Not one of the neighbours knew how the new-born baby was shaped—they saw only the large head and big, motionless eyes in a yellow face. Previously she had been healthy, alert and cheerful and able not only to struggle persistently with necessity herself but knowing also how to say a word of encouragement to others. But now it was noticed that she had become silent, that she was always musing, and knitting her brows, and looked at everything as through a mist of sorrow, with a strange, wistful, searching expression.

Little time was needed for everyone to learn about her misfortune: the child born to her was a freak, that is why she hid it, that is what depressed her.

The neighbours told her, of course, how shameful it is for a woman to be the mother of a freak; no one except the Madonna knows whether this cruel insult is a punishment justly deserved or not; but that the child was guiltless, and she was wrong to deprive it of sunshine.

She listened to them and showed them her son. His arms and legs were short, like the fins of a fish, his head, which was puffed out like a huge ball, was weakly supported by a thin, skinny neck, and his face was wrinkled like that of an old man; he had a pair of dull eyes and a large mouth drawn into a set smile.

The women cried when they beheld him, men frowned, expressed loathing and went gloomily away; the freak's mother sat on the ground, now bowing her head, now raising it and looking at the others, as if silently inquiring about something which no one could grasp.

The neighbours made a box like a coffin for the freak, and filled it with rags and combings of wool; they put the little child into this soft warm nest and placed the box out in the yard in the shade, entertaining a secret hope that the sunlight which performs miracles every day might work yet one miracle more.

Time passed, but he remained unchanged, with a large head, a thin body, and four helpless limbs; only his smile assumed a more definite expression of ravenous greed, and his mouth was becoming filled with two rows of sharp, crooked teeth. The short paws learnt to catch chunks of bread and to carry them, with rarely a mistake, to the large warm mouth.

He was dumb, but when food was being consumed near him and he could smell it he made a mumbling sound, working his jaws and shaking his large head, and the dull whites of his eyes became covered with a red network of bloody veins.

The freak's appetite was enormous, and waxed greater as time went on; his mumbling never ceased. The mother worked untiringly, but very often her earnings were small and sometimes she earned nothing at all. She did not complain, and accepted help from the neighbours rather unwillingly, and always without a word. When she was away from home the neighbours, irritated by the mumbling of the child, ran into the yard and shoved crusts of bread, vegetables, fruit, anything that could be eaten, into the ever-hungry jaws.

"Soon he will devour everything you have," they said to her. "Why don't you send him to some orphanage or hospital?"

She answered gloomily:

"Leave him alone! I am his mother, I gave him life and I must feed him."

She was fair to look upon, and more than one man sought her love, but unsuccessfully. To one whom she liked more than the rest she said:

"I cannot be your wife; I am afraid of giving birth to another freak; you would be ashamed. No, go away!"

The man tried to persuade her, reminded her of the Madonna, who is just to mothers and looks upon them as her sisters, but the freak's mother replied to him:

"I don't know what I am guilty of, but I have been cruelly punished."

He implored, wept, raged; and finally she said:

"One cannot do what one does not believe to be right. Go away!"

He went away to a far-off place and she never saw him again.

And so for many years she filled the insatiable jaws, which chewed incessantly. He devoured the fruits of her toil, her blood, her life; his head grew and became more terrible, until it seemed ready to break away from the thin weak neck and to rise in the air like a balloon; one could imagine it in its course knocking against the corners of houses, and swaying lazily from side to side.

All who looked into the yard stopped involuntarily and shuddered, unable to understand what they saw. Near the vine-covered wall, propped up on stones, as on an altar, was a box, out of which rose a head, showing up clearly against the background of foliage. The yellow, freckled, wrinkled face, with its high cheekbones, and vacant eyes starting out of their sockets, impressed itself on the memory of all who saw it; the broad flat nostrils quivered, the abnormally developed cheek-bones and jaws worked monotonously, the fleshy lips hung loose, disclosing two rows of ravenous teeth; the large projecting ears, like those of an animal, seemed to lead a separate existence. And this awful visage was crowned by a mass of black hair growing in small, close curls, like the wool of a negro.

Holding in his little hands, which were short and small like the paws of a lizard, a chunk of something to eat, the freak would bend his head forward like a bird pecking, and, wrenching off bits of food with his teeth, would munch noisily and snuffle. When he was satisfied he grinned; his eyes shifted towards the bridge of his nose, forming one dull, expressionless spot on the half-dead face, the movements of which recalled to mind the twitchings of a person in agony. When he was hungry he would crane his neck forward, open his red maw and mumble clamorously, moving a thin, snake-like tongue.

Crossing themselves and muttering a prayer people stepped aside, reminded of everything evil that they had lived through, of all the misfortunes they had experienced in their lives.

The blacksmith, an old man of a gloomy disposition, said more than once:

"When I see the all-devouring mouth of this creature I feel that somebody like him has devoured my strength; it seems to me that we all live and die for the sake of such parasites."

This dumb head called forth in everyone sombre thoughts and feelings that oppressed the heart.

The freak's mother listened to what people said, and was silent; but her hair turned quickly grey, wrinkles appeared on her face and she had long since forgotten how to laugh. It was known that sometimes she would spend the whole night standing in the doorway, and looking up at the sky as if waiting for something. Shrugging their shoulders they said to one another:

"Whatever is she waiting for?"

"Put him on the square near the old church," her neighbours advised her. "Foreigners pass there; they will be sure to throw him a few coppers."

The mother shuddered as if in horror, saying:

"It would be terrible if he were seen by strangers, by people from other countries—what would they think of us?"

They replied:

"There is misfortune everywhere, and they all know it."

Disparagingly she shook her head.

But foreigners, driven by the desire for change, wander everywhere, and naturally enough as they passed her house looked in. She was at home, she saw the ugly looks, expressing aversion and loathing, on the repleted faces of these idle people, heard how they spoke about her son, making wry mouths and screwing up their eyes. Her heart was especially wounded by a few words uttered contemptuously, with animosity, and obvious triumph.

Many times she repeated to herself the stranger's words, committing them to memory; her heart, the heart of an Italian woman and a mother, divined their insulting meaning.

That same day she went to an interpreter whom she knew and asked what the words meant.

"It depends upon who uttered them!" he replied, knitting his brows. "They mean: 'Italy is the first of the Latin races to degenerate.' ... Where did you hear this lie?"

She went away without answering.

The next day her son died in convulsions from over-eating.

She sat in the yard near the box, her hand on the head of her dead son; still seeming to be calmly waiting, waiting. She looked questioningly into the eyes of everybody who came to the house to look upon the deceased.

All were silent, no one spoke to her, though perhaps many wished to congratulate her—she had been freed from slavery—to say a word of consolation to her—she had lost a son—but everyone was mute. Sometimes people understand that there is a time for silence.

For some time after this she continued to gaze long into people's faces, as if questioning them about something; then she became as ordinary as everybody else.

THE MIGHT OF MOTHERHOOD

Let us praise Woman-Mother, the inexhaustible source of all-conquering life!

Here we shall tell of the Iron Timur-Lenk, the Lame Lynx—of Sahib-Kiran, the lucky conqueror—of Tamerlane, as the Infidels have named him—of the man who sought to destroy the whole world.

For fifty years he scoured the earth, his iron heel crushing towns and states as an elephant's foot crushes ant-hills. Red rivers of blood flowed in his tracks wherever he went. He built high towers of the bones of conquered peoples; he destroyed Life, vying with the might of Death, on whom he took revenge for having robbed him of his son Jihangir. He was a terrible man, for he wanted to deprive Death of all his victims; to leave Death to die of hunger and ennui!

From the day on which his son Jihangir died and the people of Samarcand, clothed in black and light blue, their heads covered with dust and ashes, met the conqueror of the cruel Getes, from that day until the hour when Death met him in Otrar, and overcame him—for thirty years Timur did not smile. He lived with lips compressed, bowing his head to no one, and his heart was closed to compassion for thirty years.

Let us praise Woman-Mother, the only power to which Death humbly submits. Here we shall tell the true tale of a mother, how Iron Tamerlane, the servant and slave of Death, and the bloody scourge of the earth, bowed down before her.

This is how it came to pass. Timur-Bek was feasting in the beautiful valley of Canigula which is covered with clouds of roses and jasmine, in the valley called "Love of Flowers" by the poets of Samarcand, from which one can see the light blue minarets of the great town, and the blue cupolas of the mosques.

Fifteen hundred round tents were spread out fan-wise in the valley, looking like so many tulips. Above them hundreds of silk flags were gently swaying, like living flowers.

In their midst, like a queen among her subjects, was the tent of Gurgan-Timur. The tent had four sides, each measuring one hundred paces, three spears' length in height; its roof rested on twelve golden columns as thick as the body of a man. The tent was made of silk, striped in black, yellow and light blue; five hundred red cords fastened it to the ground. There was a silver eagle at each of the four corners, and under the blue cupola, on a dais in the middle of the tent, was seated a fifth eagle—the all-conquering Timur-Gurgan himself, the King of Kings.

He wore a loose robe of light blue silk covered with no fewer than five thousand large pearls. On his grey head, which was terrible to look upon, was a white cap with a ruby on the sharp point. The ruby swayed backwards and forwards; it glistened like a fiery eye surveying the world.

The face of the Lame One was like a broad knife covered with rust from the blood into which it had been plunged thousands of times. His eyes were narrow and small but they saw everything; their gleam resembled the cold gleam of "Tsaramut," the favourite stone of the Arabs, which the infidels call emerald, and by means of which epilepsy can be cured.

The king wore earrings of rubies from Ceylon which resembled in colour a pretty girl's lips.

On the ground, on carpets that could not be matched, were three hundred golden pitchers of wine and everything needed for the royal banquet. Behind Timur stood the musicians; at his feet were his kindred: kings and princes and the commanders of his troops; by his side was no one. Nearest of all to him was the tipsy poet Kermani, he who once to the question of the destroyer of the world, "Kermani, how much would you give for me if I were to be sold?" replied to the sower of death and terror:

"Twenty-five askers."

"But that is the value of my belt alone!" exclaimed Timur, surprised.

"I was only thinking of the belt," replied Kermani, "only of the belt; because you yourself are not worth a farthing!"

Thus spake the poet Kermani to the King of Kings, to the man of evil and terror. Let us therefore value the fame of the poet, the friend of truth, always higher than the fame of Timur. Let us praise poets who have only one God—the beautifully spoken, fearless word of truth—that which is their god for ever!

It was an hour of mirth, carousal and proud reminiscences of battles and victories. Amid the sounds of music and popular games, warriors were fencing before the tent of the king, and endeavouring to show their prowess in killing. A number of motley-coloured clowns were tumbling about, strong men were wrestling, acrobats were performing as though they had no bones in their bodies. A performance of elephants was also in progress; they were painted red and green, which made some of them look ludicrous, others terrible. At this hour of joy, when Timur's men were intoxicated with fear before him, with pride in his fame, with the fatigue of battles, with wine and koumiss—at this mad hour, suddenly through the noise, like lightning through a cloud, the cry of a woman reached the ears of the conqueror of the Sultan Bayazet, the cry of a proud eagle, a sound familiar and attuned to his afflicted soul—afflicted by Death, and therefore so cruel to mankind and to life.

He gave orders to inquire who had cried out in this voice devoid of joy. He was told that a woman had come, all in rags and covered with dust; she seemed crazy, and speaking Arabic demanded—she demanded—to see the master of three parts of the world.

"Lead her in!" said the king.

Before him stood a woman, barefooted, in rags faded by the sun. Her black hair hung loose, covering her naked breast, and her face was of the colour of bronze. Her eyes expressed command and her tawny hand did not shake as she pointed it at the "Lame One."

"Are you he that defeated Sultan Bayazet?" she asked.

"Yes, I am he. I have conquered many and am not yet tired of victories. What have you to tell me about yourself, woman?"

"Listen," she said. "Whatever you may have done, you are only a man, but I am a mother. You serve Death—I serve Life. You are guilty before me and I am come to demand that you atone for your guilt. They tell me that your watchword is 'Justice is Power.' I do not believe it, but you must be just to me because I am a mother."

The king was wise enough to overlook the insult and felt the force of the words behind it. He said:

"Sit down and speak. I will listen to you."

She settled herself comfortably on a carpet in the narrow circle of kings and related as follows:—

"I have come from near Salerno. It is in far-off Italy—you would not know it. My father was a fisherman, my husband also; he was as handsome as he was happy. It was I who made him happy. I also had a son who was the finest boy in the world——"

"Like my Jihangir," said the old warrior quietly.

"My son was the finest and cleverest boy. He was six years old when Saracen pirates came to our shore. They killed my father and my husband, and many others. They kidnapped my son and for four years I have searched for him all over the earth. He must be with you now; I know it, because Bayazet's warriors captured the pirates; you defeated Bayazet and took away all he had; therefore you must know where my son is, you must give him back to me!"

"She is insane," said the kings and friends of Timur, his princes and marshals; and they all laughed, for kings always account themselves wise.

But Kermani looked seriously at the woman, and Tamerlane seemed greatly astonished.

"She is as insane as a mother," quietly said the poet Kermani; but the king—the enemy of the world—replied:

"Woman, how came you from that unknown country, across the seas, across rivers and mountains, through the forests? How is it that wild beasts, and men, who are often more ferocious than the wildest of beasts, did not harm you? You came even without a weapon, the only friend of the defenceless that does not betray them as long as they have strength in their arms. I must know it all in order that I may believe you and in order that my astonishment may not prevent me from understanding you."

Let us praise Woman-Mother, whose love knows no bounds, by whose breast the whole world has been nourished. Everything that is beautiful in man comes from the rays of the sun and from mother's milk; these are the sources of our love of life.

The woman replied to Timur-Lenk:

"I came across one sea only, a sea with many islands, where I found fishermen's boats. When one is seeking what one loves the wind is always favourable. For one who has been born and bred by the seashore it is easy to swim across rivers. Mountains? I saw no mountains."

"A mountain becomes a valley when one loves!" interjected smilingly the poet Kermani.

"True, there were forests on the way. There were wild boars, bears, lynxes and terrible-looking bulls that lowered their heads threateningly; twice lynxes stared at me with eyes like yours. But every beast has a heart. I talked to them as I talk to you. They believed me that I was a mother and went away sighing. They pitied me. Know you not that beasts also love their young, and will fight for the life and freedom of those they love as valiantly as men?"

"That is true, woman," said Timur. "Very often, I know, their love is stronger and they fight harder than men."

"Men," she continued like a child, for every mother is a hundred times a child in her soul, "men are always children of their mothers, for everyone has a mother, everyone is somebody's son, even you, old man; a woman bore you. You may renounce God, but that you cannot renounce, old man."

"That is true, woman," exclaimed Kermani, the fearless poet. "You can have no calves from a herd of bulls, no flowers bloom without the sun, there is no happiness without love. There is no love without woman. There is no poet or hero without a mother."

And the woman said:

"Give me back my child, because I am a mother and I love him!"

Let us bow down before Woman—she gave birth to Moses, Mahomet, and the Great Prophet Jesus who was murdered by the wicked, but who, as Sherif-eddin said, "will rise and come to judge the living and the dead. It will happen in Damascus."

Let us bow down before her who through the centuries gives birth to great men. Aristotle was her son, and Firdousi, and honey-sweet Saadi, and Omar Khayyam that is like wine mixed with poison, Iscander and blind Homer. All these are her children, they all have drunk her milk and every one of them was led into the world by her hand—when they were no taller than a tulip. All the pride of the world is due to mothers.

And the grey destroyer of towns, the lame tiger Timur-Gurgan, grew thoughtful and for a long time was silent. Then to all present he said:

"Men Tangri Kuli, Timur (I, Timur, a servant of God) say what I must say. I have lived for many years and the earth groans under me. For thirty years, with this hand of mine, I have been destroying the harvest of Death, I have been taking revenge upon Death because Death put out the sun of my heart—robbed me of my Jihangir. Others have struggled for cities and for kingdoms, but none has so striven for a man. Men had no value in my eyes; I cared not who they were nor why they were in my way. It was I, Timur, who said to Bayazet when I had defeated him: 'O Bayazet, it seems that kingdoms are nothing before God; you see that He gives them into the hands of people like us—you who are a cripple and me who am lame!' I said this to him when he was led up to me in chains, groaning under their weight. I looked upon his misfortune and felt that love was bitter as wormwood, the weed that grows on ruins.

"A servant of God, I say what I must. A woman sits before me, her number is legion and she has awakened in my soul feelings hitherto unknown to me. As an equal she speaks to me and she does not ask, she demands. I see and understand why this woman is so powerful: she loves and love helped her to recognise that her child is the spark of life from which a flame may spring that will burn for many centuries. Have not all prophets been children, and all heroes been weak? O Jihangir, the light of my eyes, perhaps it was thy lot to warm the earth, to sow happiness on it: I have covered it well with blood and made it fertile."

Again the Scourge of Nations pondered long. At last he said:

"I, Timur, slave of God, say what I must. Let three hundred horsemen go to all the four corners of my kingdom and let them find this woman's son. She shall wait here and I will wait with her. Happy shall he be who returns with the child on his saddle. Woman, is that right?"

She tossed her black hair from her face, smiled at him and, nodding, answered:

"Quite right, O king!"
Then the terrible old man rose and bowed to her in silence, but the merry poet Kermani sang joyfully like a child:

"What is more delightful than a song of flowers and stars?
Everyone will say: a song of love.
What is more enchanting than the midday sun in May?
A lover will reply: she whom I love.
Ah, I know the stars are splendid in the sky at depth of night,
And I know the sun is gorgeous on a dazzling summer's day,
But the eyes of my beloved out-rival all the flowers,
And her smile is more entrancing than the sun in May.
But no one yet has sung the best, most charming song of all;
Tis the song of all beginnings, of the heart of all the world,
Of the magic heart of women, and the mother of us all!"

Timur-Lenk said to his poet:

"Quite right, Kermani! God did not err when He selected your lips to announce his wisdom!"

"Well, God himself is a good poet!" said the drunken Kermani.

And the woman smiled, and all the kings and princes and warriors smiled too, like children, as they looked at her—the Woman-Mother.

All this is true. What is said here is the truth, all mothers know it, ask them and they will say:

"Yes, all this is everlasting truth. We are more powerful than Death, we who ceaselessly present sages, poets and heroes to the world, we who sow in it everything that is glorious!"

A MESSAGE FROM THE SEA

It is as if thousands of metallic wires were strung in the thick foliage of the olive-trees. The wind moves the stiff, hard leaves, they touch the strings, and these light, continuous contacts fill the air with a hot, intoxicating sound. It is not yet music, but a sound as if unseen hands were tuning hundreds of invisible harps, and one awaits impatiently the moment of silence before a powerful hymn bursts forth, a hymn to the sun, the sky and the sea, played on numberless stringed instruments.

The wind sways the tops of the trees, which seem to be moving down the mountain slope towards the sea. The waves beat in a measured, muffled way against the stones on the shore. The sea is covered with moving white spots, as if numberless flocks of birds had settled on its blue expanse; they all swim in the same direction, disappear, diving into the depths, and reappear, giving forth a faint sound. On the horizon, looking like grey birds, move two ships under full sail, dragging the other birds in their train. All this reminds one of a half-forgotten dream seen long ago; it is so unlike reality.

"The wind will freshen towards evening," says an old fisherman, sitting on a little mound of jingling pebbles in the shade of the rocks.

The breakers have washed up on to the stones a tangle of smelling seaweed—brown and golden and green; the wrack withers in the sun and on the hot stones, the salt air is saturated with the penetrating odour of iodine. One after another the curling breakers beat upon the heap of shingle.

The old fisherman resembles a bird: he has a small pinched face and an aquiline nose; his eyes, which are almost hidden in the folds of the skin, are small and round, though probably keen enough. His fingers are like crooks, bony and stiff.

"Half-a-century ago, signor," said the old man, in a tone that was in harmony with the beating of the waves and the chirping of the crickets—it was just such another day as this, gladsome and noisy, with everything laughing and singing. My father was forty, I was sixteen, and in love of course—it is inevitable when one is sixteen and the sun is bright.

"'Let us go, Guido, and catch some pezzoni,' said my father to me. Pezzoni, signor, are very thin and tasty fish with pink fins; they are also called coral fish because they live at a great depth where coral is found. To catch them one has to cast anchor, and angle with a hook attached to a heavy weight. It is a pretty fish.

"And we set off, looking forward to naught but a good catch. My father was a strong man, an experienced fisherman, but just then he had been ailing, his chest hurt him, and his fingers were contracted with rheumatism—he had worked on a cold winter's day and caught the fisherman's complaint.

"The wind here is very tricky and mischievous, the kind of wind that sometimes breathes on you from the shore as if gently pushing you into the sea; and at another time will creep up to you unawares and then rush at you as if you had offended it. The boat breaks loose and flies before it, sometimes with keel uppermost, with you yourself in the water. All this happens in a moment, you have no chance either to curse or to mention God's name, as you are whirled and driven far out to sea. A highwayman is more honourable than this kind of wind. But then, signor, human beings are always more honourable than elemental forces.

"Yes, this wind pounced upon us when we were three miles from the shore—quite close, you see, but it struck us as unexpectedly as a coward or a scoundrel. 'Guido,' said my father, clutching at the oars with his crippled hands. 'Hold on, Guido! Be quick—weigh anchor!'

"While I was weighing the anchor my father was struck in the chest by one of the oars and fell stunned into the bottom of the boat. I had no time to help him, signor; every second we might capsize. Events moved quickly: when I got hold of the oars, we were rushing along rapidly, surrounded by the dust-like spray of the water; the wind picked off the tops of the waves and sprinkled us like a priest, only with more zest, signor, and without any desire to wash away our sins.

"'This is a bad look-out!' said my father when he came to, and had taken a look in the direction of the shore. 'It will soon be all over, my son.'

"When one is young one does not readily believe in danger; I tried to row, did all that one can do on the water in such a moment of danger, when the wind, like the breath of wicked devils, amiably digs thousands of graves for you and sings the requiems for nothing.

"'Sit still, Guido,' said my father, grinning and shaking the water off his head. 'What is the use of poking the sea with match-sticks? Save your strength, my son; otherwise they will wait in vain for you at home.'

"The green waves toss out little boat as children toss a ball, peer at us over the boat's sides, rise above our heads, roar, shake, drop us into deep pits. We rise again on the white crests, but the coast runs farther and farther away from us and seems to dance like our boat. Then my father said to me:

"'Maybe you will return to land, but I—never. Listen and I will tell you something about a fisherman's work.'

"And he began to tell me all he knew of the habits of the different kinds of fishes: where, when and how best to catch them.

"'Should we not rather pray, father?' I asked him when I realised that our plight was desperate; we were like a couple of rabbits amidst a pack of white hounds which grinned at us on all sides.

"'God sees everything,' he said. 'If he sees everything He knows that men who were created for the land are now perishing in the sea, and that one of them, hoping to be saved, wishes to tell Him what he, the Father, already knows. It is not prayer but work that the earth and the people need. God understands that.'

"And having told me everything he knew about work my father began to talk about how one should live with others.

"'Is this the proper time to teach me?' said I. 'You did not do it when we were on shore.'

"'On shore I did not feel the proximity of death so.'

"The wind howled like a wild beast and furiously lashed the waves; my father had to shout to make me hear.

"'Always act as if there lived no one better and no one worse than yourself—that will always be right! A landowner and a fisherman, a priest and a soldier, belong to one body; you are needed just as much as any other of its members. Never approach a man with the idea that there is more bad in him than good; get to think that the good outweighs the bad and it will be so. People give what is asked of them.'"

"These things were not said all at once, of course, but intermittently, like words of command. We were tossed from wave to wave, and the words came to me sometimes from below, sometimes from above through the spray. Much of what he said was carried off before it reached my ear, much I could not understand: is it a time to learn, signor, when every minute you are threatened with death! I was in great fear; it was the first time that I had seen the sea in such a rage, and I felt utterly helpless. The sensation is still vivid in my memory, but I cannot tell whether I experienced it then or afterwards when I recalled those hours.

"As if it were now I see my father: he sits at the bottom of the boat, his feeble arms outstretched, his hands gripping the sides of the boat; his hat has been washed away; from right and left, from fore and aft, the waves are breaking over his head and shoulders.... He shook his head, sniffed and shouted to me from time to time. He was wet through and looked very small, and fear, or perhaps it was pain, had made his eyes large. I think it was pain.

"'Listen!' he shouted to me. 'Do you hear?'

"'At times,' I replied to him, 'I hear.'

"'Remember that everything that is good comes from man.'

"'I will remember!' I replied.

"He had never spoken to me in this way on land. He had been jovial and kindly, but it seemed to me that he regarded me with a lack of confidence and a sort of contempt—I was still a child for him; sometimes it offended me, for in youth one's pride is strong.

"His shouts must have lessened my fear, for I remember it all very clearly." The old fisherman remained silent for a while, looking at the white sea and smiling; then with a wink he said:

"As I have observed men, I know that to remember means to understand, and the more you understand the more good you see; that is quite true, believe me.

"Yes, I remember his wet face that was so dear to me, and his big eyes that looked at me so earnestly, so lovingly, and in such a way that somehow I knew at the time that I was not going to perish on that day. I was frightened, but I knew that I should not perish.

"Our boat capsized, of course, and we were in the swirling water, in the blinding foam, hedged in by sharp-crested waves, which tossed our bodies about, and battered them against the keel of the boat. We had fastened ourselves to the boat with everything that could be tied, and were holding on by ropes. As long as our strength lasted we should not be torn away from our boat, but it was difficult to keep afloat. Several times he and I were tossed on to the keel and then washed off again. The worst of it is, signor, that you become dizzy, and deaf and blind—the water gets into your eyes and ears and you swallow a lot of it.

"This lasted long—for full seven hours—and then the wind suddenly changed, blew towards the coast and swept us along with it. I was overjoyed and shouted:

"'Hold on!'

"My father also cried out, but I understood only:

"'They will smash us.'

"He meant the stones, but they were still far off; I did not believe him. But he understood matters better than I: we rushed along amid mountains of water, clinging like snails to our 'mother who fed us.' The waves had battered our bodies, dashed us against the boat and we already felt exhausted and benumbed. So we went on for a long time; but when once the dark mountains came in sight everything moved with lightning speed. The mountains seemed to reel as they came towards us, to bend over the water as if about to tumble on our heads. One, two! The white waves toss up our bodies, our boat crackles like a nut under the heel of a boot; I am torn away from it, I see the broken ribs of the rocks, like sharp knives, like the devil's claws, and I see my father's head high above me. He was found on the rocks two days later, with his back broken and his skull smashed. The wound in the head was large, part of the brain had been washed out. I remember the grey particles intermingled with red sinews in the wound, like marble or foam streaked with blood. He was terribly mutilated, all broken, but his face was uninjured and calm, and his eyes were tightly closed.

"And I? Yes, I also was badly mangled. They dragged me on to the shore unconscious. We were carried to the mainland beyond Amalfi—a place unknown to us, but the people there were also fishermen, our own kith and kin. Cases like ours do not surprise them, but render them kind; people who lead a dangerous life are always kind!

"I fear I have not spoken to you as I feel about my father, and of what I have kept in my heart for fifty-one years. Special words may be required to do that, even a song; but we are simple folk, like fishes, and are unable to speak as prettily and expressively as one would wish! One always feels and knows more than one is able to tell.

"What is most striking about the whole matter is that, although my father knew that the hour of his death had come, he did not get frightened or forget me, his son. He found time and strength to tell me all he considered important. I have lived sixty-seven years and I can say that everything he imparted to me is true!"

The old man took off his knitted cap, which had once been red but had faded, and pulled a pipe out of it. Then, inclining his bald bronzed skull to one side, he said with emphasis:

"It is all true, dear signor! People are just as you like to see them; look at them with kind eyes and all will be well with you, and with them, too; it will make them still better, and you too! It is very simple!"

The wind freshens considerably, the waves become higher, sharper and whiter, birds appear on the sea and fly swiftly away, disappearing in the distance. The two ships with their outspread sails have passed beyond the blue streak of the horizon.

The steep banks of the island are edged with lace-like foam, the blue water splashes angrily, and the crickets chirp on with never a pause.

THE HONOUR OF THE VILLAGE

"On the day when this happened the sirocco was blowing—a hot wind from Africa, and a nasty wind, too! It irritates one's nerves and puts one in a bad temper! That is probably the reason why the two carters, Giuseppe Cirotta and Luigi Meta, were quarrelling. No one knew how the quarrel began. No one knew who began it. All that people saw was that Luigi had thrown himself upon Giuseppe and was trying to clutch his throat; while the latter, his shoulders hunched to protect his head and his thick red neck, was making a lusty use of his strong black fists.

"They were separated and asked:

"'What is the matter?'

"Quite purple with anger Luigi exclaimed:

"'Let this bull repeat in the presence of everybody what he said about my wife!'

"Cirotta tried to get away. His small eyes hidden in the folds of a disdainful grimace, he shook his black bullet head, and stubbornly refused to repeat the offending words. Meta then shouted out in a loud voice:

"'He says that he has known the sweetness of my wife's caresses!'

"'H'm,' said the people, 'this is no joking matter; this requires serious attention. Be calm, Luigi. You are a stranger in our parts; your wife belongs here. We all knew her as a child, and if you have been wronged her guilt falls equally on all of us. Let us be outspoken!'

"They all gathered round Cirotta.

"'Did you say it?'

"'Well, yes, I did,' he admitted.

"'And is it the truth?'

"'Who has ever known me tell a lie?'

"Cirotta was a respectable man—a husband and a father; the matter was taking a very serious turn. Those present were perplexed and seemed to be thinking hard. Luigi went home and said to Concetta:

"'I am going away! I don't want you any more unless you can prove that the words of this scoundrel are a calumny.'

"Of course she began to cry, but then tears do not acquit one: Luigi pushed her away. She would be left with a child in her arms without food or money.

"Catherine was the first of the women to intervene. She kept a small greengrocer's shop and was as cunning as a fox; in appearance she resembled an old sack filled unevenly with flesh and bones.

"'Signor,' she said, 'you have already heard that this concerns the honour of us all. It is not a prank prompted by a night when the moon is bright; the fate of two mothers is involved, isn't that so? I will take Concetta to my house and let her live with me till we find out the truth.'

"She was as good as her word; and later she and Luccia, the noisy, shrivelled old witch, whose voice could be heard three miles away, both tackled poor Giuseppe: they asked him to come out and began to pluck at his soul as if it had been an old rag.

"'Well, my good man, tell us how many times you took Concetta to yourself?'

"The fat Giuseppe puffed out his cheeks, thought awhile, and said:

"'Once!'

"'He could have told us that without reflection,' remarked Luccia aloud, as if talking to herself.

"'Did it happen in the evening, in the night, or in the morning?' asked Catherine, after the fashion of a judge.

"Giuseppe chose evening without thinking.

"'Was it still daylight?'

"'Yes,' said the fool.

"'That means that you saw her body?'

"'Yes, of course.'

"'Then tell us what it looked like.'

"He understood at last the drift of the questions, and opened his mouth like a sparrow choking with a grain of barley. He understood, and muttered angrily under his breath; blood rushed to his large ears till they became quite purple.

"'Well, what can I say? I did not examine her like a doctor!'

"'You eat fruit without enjoying the look of it?' asked Luccia. 'But perhaps you noticed one of Concetta's peculiarities?' She went on questioning him, laughing and winking as she did so.

"'It all happened so quickly,' said Giuseppe, 'that, to tell you the truth, I didn't notice anything.'

"'That means that you never had her,' said Catherine.

"She was a kind woman, but, when necessary, she could be quite stern. In the end, they so confused the fellow and made him contradict himself so often that he lost his head—and confessed:

"'Nothing at all happened; I said it simply out of malice.'

"This did not surprise the old women.

"'It is what we thought,' they said; and, letting him go, they left the matter to the decision of the men.

"Two days later our Workers' Society met. Cirotta had to face them, having been accused of libelling a woman. Old Giacomo Fasca, a blacksmith, said in a way that did credit to him:

"'Citizens, comrades and good people! We demand that justice shall be done to us. We on our part must be just to everybody: let everybody understand that we know the high value of what we want, and that justice is not an empty word for us as it is for our masters. Here is a man who has libelled a woman, offended a comrade, disrupted one family and brought sorrow to another, who has made his wife suffer jealousy and shame. Our attitude to this man should be stern. What do you propose to do?'

"Sixty-seven tongues exclaimed in one voice:

"'Drive him out of the commune!'

"Fifteen of the men thought that this was too severe a punishment, and a dispute arose. And the dispute became a very noisy one, for the fate of a man hung on their decision, and not the fate of one man only: the man was married and had three children. What had his wife and children done? He had a house, a vineyard, a pair of horses, four donkeys for the use of foreigners. All these things had been acquired by his own labour and had cost him a deal of pains. Poor Giuseppe was skulking in a corner amongst the children and looked as gloomy as the very devil. He sat doubled up on a chair, his head bowed, fumbling his hat. He had pulled off the ribbon already, and now was slowly tearing off the brim. His fingers jerked as if he were playing the fiddle. When he was asked what he had to say he stood up slowly and, straightening his body, said:

"'I beg you to be lenient! There is no one without sin. To drive me off the land on which I have lived for more than thirty years, and where my ancestors have worked, would not be just.'

"The women were also against his being exiled, so Giacomo Fasca at last made the following proposal:—

"'I think, friends, that he will be sufficiently punished if we saddle

him with the duty of keeping Luigi's wife and child—let him pay
her half as much as Luigi earned!'

"They discussed the matter at great length and finally settled on
that. Giuseppe Cirotta was very pleased to get off so easily. Besides,
this decision satisfied all: the matter was not taken into the law
courts, it was decided in their own circle and no knives were used.

"We do not like, signor, what they write about our affairs in the
papers in a language unfamiliar to us. The words that we can
understand occur only here and there, like teeth in an old man's
mouth. Besides, we don't like the way the judges talk of us, for they
are strangers to us and don't understand our life. They talk of us as
if we were savages and they themselves angels of God, who don't
know the taste of meat or wine, and don't touch womenkind. We
are simple folks and we look on life in a simple way.

"So they decided that Giuseppe Cirotta should keep the wife and
child of Luigi Meta.

"The matter however had a different ending.

"When Luigi found out that Cirotta's words were untrue and that
his wife was innocent, and when he heard our decision, he wrote
her a short note in which he invited her to come home:

*

"'Come to me and we shall live happily again. Do not take a
farthing from that man and, if you have taken any, throw it in his
face! I am guilty before you. Could I have thought that a man
would lie in such a matter as love?'

*

"But he also wrote another letter to Cirotta:

"'I have three brothers and all four of us have sworn to one another
that we will kill you like a ram if you ever leave the island and land
in Sorrento, Castellamare, Torre, or anywhere else. As soon as we

63

find it out we shall kill you, remember! This is as true as that we belong to your commune and are good honest people. My wife has no need of your help. Even my pig would refuse to eat your bread. Do not leave this island until I tell you you may!'

"That is how it all happened. It is said that Cirotta took this letter to the judge and asked him whether Luigi could not be punished for threatening him, and that the judge said:

"'Of course he can, but then his brothers will certainly kill you; they will come over here and kill you. I advise you to wait. That is better. Anger is not like love: it does not last for ever!'

"The judge may have said it: he is a good and clever man, and makes very good verses; but I don't believe that Cirotta ever went to him or showed him the letter. No, Cirotta is a decent fellow and it is not likely that he would have acted so stupidly. People would have jeered at him.

"We are simple working people, signor. We have our own life, our own ideas and opinions. We have a right to shape our life as we like and as we think best.

"Socialists? Friend, in my opinion a working man is born a socialist; although we don't read books we can smell the truth—truth has a strong smell about it which is always the same—the smell of the sweat of labour!"

THE SOCIALIST

Before the door of a white canteen hidden among the thick vines of an old vineyard, in the shade of a canopy of vine branches interspersed with morning glory and small Chinese roses, at a table on which stood a decanter of wine, sat Vincenzo, a painter, with Giovanni, a locksmith. The painter is a small man, thin and dark; his eyes are lit with the soft, musing smile of a dreamer. His upper lip and cheeks have the appearance of having been recently shaved, but his smile makes him look very young, almost childlike. He has a small, pretty mouth like that of a girl; his wrists are slender, and in his nimble fingers he twists a yellow rose, pressing it to his full lips and closing his eyes.

"Perhaps so. I don't know; perhaps so," he says quietly, shaking his head, which has hollows at the temples. Dark curls fall over his high forehead.

"Yes, yes, the farther north one goes the more persistent are the people," asserts Giovanni, a broad-shouldered fellow with a large head and black curls. His face is copper-coloured, his nose sunburnt and covered with white scales of dead skin. His eyes are large and gentle like those of an ox, and there is a finger missing from his left hand. His speech is as slow as the movements of his hands, which are stained with oil and iron dust. Grasping his wineglass in his dark fingers, the nails of which are chipped and broken, he continues in his deep voice:

"Milan, Turin—there are splendid workshops there in which new people are being made, where a new brain is growing. Wait a little while and the world will become honest and wise!"

"Yes," said the little painter; and he lifted his glass, trying to catch a sunbeam in the wine, and sang:

> "When we are young
> How high the heart aspires!

How Time hath slaked its fires
When we are old!"

"The farther north one goes, I say, the better is the work. The French, for instance, do not lead such a lazy life as we do. Farther on, there are the Germans, and last of all the Russians: they are men if you like!"

"Quite true."

"Having no rights and no fear of being deprived of their freedom and life, they have done grand work: it is owing to them that the whole East has awakened to life."

"The county of heroes," said the painter, inclining his head. "I should like to live amongst them."

"Would you?" exclaimed the locksmith, striking his knee with his fist. "You would turn into a piece of ice there in a week!"

They both laughed good humouredly.

Around them there are blue and golden flowers; sunbeams tremble in the air; in the transparent glass of the decanter and the tumblers the wine seems to be on fire. From afar comes the soft murmur of the sea.

"Well, my good Vincenzo," said the locksmith, with a broad smile. "Tell me in verse how I became a socialist. Do you know how it happened?"

"No," said the painter, filling the glasses with wine and smiling at the red stream. "You have never told me. This skin fits your bones so well that I thought you were born in it!"

"I was born naked and stupid, like you and everybody else; in my youth I dreamed of a rich wife; when I was a soldier I studied in order to pass the examination for an officer's rank. I was twenty-three when I felt that all was not as it should be in this world, and that it was a shame to live as if it were, like a fool."

The painter rested his elbows on the table and, raising his head, gazed at the mountains where, on the very edge of the precipice, moving their large branches, stood huge pine-trees.

"We, our whole regiment, were sent to Bologna. The peasantry there were in revolt, some demanding that the rent of land should be lowered, others shouting about the necessity for raising wages: both parties seemed to be in the wrong. 'To lower rents and increase wages, what nonsense!' thought I. 'That would ruin the landowners.' To me, who was a town-dweller, it seemed utter foolishness. I was very indignant—the heat helped to make one so, and the constant travelling from place to place and the mounting guard at night. For, you know, these fine fellows were breaking the machinery belonging to the landowners; and it pleased them to burn the corn and to try to spoil everything that did not belong to them. Just think of it!"

He sipped his wine and, becoming more animated, went on:

"They roamed about the fields in droves like sheep, always silently, but threateningly and as if they meant business. We used to scatter them, threatening them with our bayonets sometimes. Now and then we struck them with the butts of our rifles. Without showing much fear, they dispersed in leisurely fashion, but always came together again. It was a tedious business, like mass, and it lasted for days, like an attack of fever. Luoto, our non-commissioned officer, a fine fellow from Abruzzi, himself a peasant, was anxious and troubled: he turned quite yellow and thin, and more than once he said to us:

"'It's a bad business, boys; it will probably be necessary to shoot, damn it!'

"His grumbling upset us still more; and then, you know, from every corner, from every hillock and tree we could see peeping the obstinate heads of the peasants; their angry eyes seemed to pierce us. For these people, naturally enough, did not regard us in a very friendly light."

"Drink," said little Vincenzo cordially, pushing a full glass towards his friend.

"Thank you. Long live the people who persist!" exclaimed the locksmith in his bass voice. He emptied the glass, wiped his moustache with his hands, and continued:

"Once I stood on a small hillock near an olive grove, guarding some trees which the peasants had been injuring. At the bottom of the hill two men were at work, an old man and a youth. They were digging a ditch. It was very hot, the sun burnt like fire, one felt irritable, longed to be a fish, and I remember I eyed them angrily. At noon they both left off work, and got out some bread and cheese and a jug of wine. 'Oh, devil take them!' thought I to myself. Suddenly the old man, who previously had not once looked at me, said something to the youth, who shook his head disapprovingly, but the old man shouted:

'Go on!' He said this very sternly.

"The youth came up to me with the jug in his hand, and said, not very willingly, you know:

"'My father thinks that you would like a drink and offers you some wine.'

"I felt embarrassed, but I was pleased. I refused, nodding at the same time to the old man and thanking him. He responded by looking at the sky.

"'Drink it, signor, drink it. We offer this to you as a man, not as a soldier. We do not expect a soldier to become kinder because he has drunk our wine!'

"'D—you, don't get nasty,' I thought to myself, and having drunk about three mouthfuls I thanked him. Then they began to eat down below. A little later I was relieved by Ugo from Salertino. I told him quietly that these two peasants were good fellows. The same night, as I stood at the door of a barn where the machinery was kept a slate fell on my head from the roof—it did not do much damage, but another slate, striking my shoulder edgewise, hurt me so severely that my left arm dropped benumbed."

The locksmith burst into a loud laugh, his mouth wide open, his eyes half-closed.

"Slates, stones, sticks," said he, through his laughter, "in those days and at that place were alive. This independent action of lifeless things made some pretty big bumps on our heads. Wherever a soldier stood or walked, a stick would suddenly fly at him from the ground, or a stone fall upon him from the sky. It made us savage, as you can guess."

The eyes of the little painter became sad, his face turned pale and he said quietly:

"One always feels ashamed to hear of such things."

"What is one to do? People take time to get wise. Then I called for help. I was led into a house where another fellow lay, his face cut by a stone. When I asked him how it happened he said, smiling, but not with mirth:

"'An old woman, comrade, an old grey witch struck me, and then proposed that I should kill her!'

"'Was she arrested?'

"'I said that I had done it myself, that I had fallen and hurt myself. The commander did not believe it, I could see it by his eyes. But, don't you see, it was awkward to confess that I had been wounded by an old woman. Eh? The devil! Of course they are hard pressed and one can understand that they do not love us!'

"'H'm!' thought I. The doctor came and two ladies with him, one of them fair and very pretty, evidently a Venetian. I don't remember the other. They looked at my wound. It was slight, of course. They applied a poultice and went away."

The locksmith frowned, became silent and rubbed his hands hard; his companion filled the glasses again with wine; as he lifted the decanter the wine seemed to dance in the air like a live red fire.

"We used both to sit at the window," continued the locksmith darkly. "We sat in such a way that the light did not fall on us, and there once we heard the charming voice of this fair lady. She and her companion were walking with the doctor in the garden outside the window and talking in French, which I understand very well.

"'Did you notice the colour of his eyes?' she asked. 'He is a peasant of course, and once he has taken off his uniform will no doubt become a socialist, like they all are here. People with eyes like that want to conquer the whole world, to reconstruct the whole of life, to drive us out, to destroy us in order that some blind, tedious justice should triumph!'

"'Foolish fellows,' said the doctor-'half children, half brutes.'

"'Brutes, that is quite true. But what is there childish about them?'

"'What about those dreams of universal equality?'

"'Yes, just imagine it. The fellow with the eyes of an ox and the other with the face of a bird our equals! You, she and I their equals, the equals of these people of inferior blood! People who can be bidden to come and kill their fellows, who are brutes like them....'

"She spoke much and vehemently. I listened and thought:

"'Quite right, signora.' I had seen her more than once, and you know of course that no one dreams more ardently of a woman than a soldier. I imagined her to be kind and clever and warmhearted; and at that time I had an idea that the landed nobility were especially clever, or gifted, or something of the kind. I don't know why!

"I asked my comrade:

"'Do you understand this language?'

"No, he did not understand. Then I translated for him the fair lady's speech. The fellow got as angry as the devil, and started to jump about the room, his one eye glistening—the other was bandaged.

"'Is that so?' he murmured. 'Is that possible? She makes use of me and does not look upon me as a man. For her sake I allow my dignity to be offended and she denies it. For the sake of guarding her property I risk losing my soul.'

"He was not a fool and felt that he had been very much insulted, and so did I. The following day we talked about this lady in a loud voice, not heeding Luoto, who only muttered:

"'Be more careful, boys; don't forget that you are soldiers, and that there is such a thing as discipline.'

"No, we did not forget it. But many of us, almost all, to tell you the truth, became deaf and blind, and these young peasants made use of our deafness and blindness to very good purpose. They won. They treated us very well indeed. The fair lady could have learnt from them: for instance, they could have taught her very convincingly how honest people should be valued. When we left the place whither we had come with the idea of shedding blood, many of us were given flowers. As we marched along the streets of the village not stones and slates but flowers were thrown at us, my friend. I think we had deserved it. One may forget a cool reception when one has received such a good send-off!"

He laughed heartily, then said:

"That is what you should turn into verse, Vincenzo."

The painter replied with a pensive smile:

"Yes, it's a good subject for a small poem. I think I may be able to do something with it. But when a man is over twenty-five he is a poor lyric poet."

He threw away the crumpled flower, picked another and, looking round, continued quietly:

"When one has covered the road from mother's breast to the breast of one's sweetheart, one must go on to another kind of happiness."

The locksmith became silent, tilting his wine in the glass.

Below them the sea murmurs softly; in the hot air above the vineyards floats the perfume of flowers.

"It is the sun that makes us so lazy and good-for-nothing," murmured the locksmith.

"I don't seem to be able to manage lyric verse satisfactorily now. I am rather sick about it," said Vincenzo quietly, knitting his thin brows.

"Have you written anything lately?"

The painter did not reply at once.

"Yes, yesterday I wrote something on the roof of the Hotel Como."

And he read in a low tone and pensive and sing-song manner:

> "The autumn sun falls softly, taking leave,
> And lights the greyness of the lonely shore.
> The greedy waves o'erlip the scattered stones
> And lick the sun into the cold blue sea.
> The autumn wind goes gleaning yellow leaves,
> To toss them idly in the blust'ring air.
> Pale is the sky, and wild the angry sea,
> The sun still faintly smiles, and sinks, and sets."

They were both silent for a time. The painter's head had sunk and his eyes were fixed on the ground. The big, burly locksmith smiled and said at last:

"One can speak in a beautiful way about everything, but what is most beautiful of all is a word about a good man, a song of good people."

THE HUNCHBACK

The sun, like a golden rain, streams down through the dark curtain of vine leaves on to the terrace of the hotel; it is as if golden threads were strung in the air.

On the grey pavement and on the white table-cloths the shadows make strange designs, and it seems as though, if one looked long at them, one might learn to read them as one reads poetry, one might learn the meaning of it all. Bunches of grapes gleam in the sun, like pearls or the strange dull stone olivine, and the water in the decanter on the table sparkles like blue diamonds.

In the passage between the tables lies a round lace handkerchief, dropped, without a doubt, by a woman divinely fair—it cannot be otherwise, one cannot think otherwise on this sultry day full of glowing poetry, a day when everything banal and commonplace becomes invisible and hides from the sun, as if ashamed of itself.

All is quiet, save for the twitter of the birds in the garden and the humming of the bees as they hover over the flowers. From the vineyards on the mountain-side the sounds of a song float on the hot air and reach the ear: the singers are a man and a woman. Each verse is separated from the others by a moment's pause, and this interval of silence lends a special expression to the song, giving it something of the character of a prayer.

A lady comes from the garden and ascends the broad marble steps; she is old and very tall. Her dark face is serious; her brows are contracted in a deep frown, and her thin lips are tightly compressed, as if she had just said:

"No!"

Round her spare shoulders is a long, broad, gold-coloured scarf edged with lace, which looks almost like a mantle. The grey hair of her little head, which is too small for her size, is covered with black lace. In one hand she carries a long-handled red sunshade, in the other a black velvet bag embroidered in silver. She walks as firmly as a soldier through the web of sunbeams, tapping the noisy pavement with the end of her sunshade.

Her profile is the very picture of sternness: her nose is aquiline and on the end of her sharp chin grows a large grey wart; her rounded forehead projects over dark hollows where, in a network of wrinkles, her eyes are hidden. They are hidden so deep that the woman appears almost blind.

On the steps behind her, swaying from side to side like a duck, appears noiselessly the square body of a hunchback with a large, heavy, forward-hanging head, covered with a grey soft hat. His hands are in the pockets of his waistcoat, which makes him look broader and more angular still. He wears a white suit and white boots with soft soles. His weak mouth is half open, disclosing prominent, yellow and uneven teeth. The dark moustache which grows on his upper lip is unsightly, for the bristles are sparse and wiry. He breathes quickly and heavily. His nostrils quiver but the moustache does not move. He moves his short legs jerkily as he walks. His large eyes gaze languidly, as if tired, at the ground; and on his small body are displayed many large things: a large gold ring with a cameo on the first finger of his left hand, a large golden charm with two rubies at the end of a black ribbon fob, and a large—a too large—opal, an unlucky stone, in his blue necktie.

A third figure follows them leisurely along the terrace. It is that of another old woman, small and round, with a kind red face and quick eyes: she is, one may guess, of an amiable and talkative disposition.

They walk across the terrace through the hotel doorway, looking like people out of a picture of Hogarth's—sad, ugly, grotesque, unlike anything else under the sun. Everything seems to grow dark and dim in their presence.

They are Dutch people, brother and sister, the children of a diamond merchant and banker. Their life has been full of strange events if one may believe what is lightly said of them.

As a child, the hunchback was quiet, self-contained, always musing, and not fond of toys. This attracted no special attention from anybody except his sister. His father and mother thought that was how a deformed boy should be; but in the girl, who was four years older than her brother, his character aroused a feeling of anxiety.

Almost every day she was with him, trying in all possible ways to awaken in him some animation. To make him laugh she would push toys towards him. He piled them one on top of another, building a sort of pyramid. Only very rarely did he reward her efforts with a forced smile; as a rule he looked at his sister, as at everything else, with a forlorn look in his large eyes which seemed to suffer from some strange kind of blindness. This look chilled her ardour and irritated her.

"Don't dare to look at me like that! You will grow up an idiot!" she shouted, stamping her foot. And she would pinch him and beat him. He whimpered and put up his long arms to guard his head, but he never ran away from her and never complained.

Later on, when she thought that he could understand what had become quite clear to her she kept saying to him:

"Since you are a freak, you must be clever, or else everybody will be ashamed of you, father, mother, and everybody! Even other people will be ashamed that in such a rich house there should be a freak. In a rich house everything must be beautiful and clever. Do you understand that?"

"Yes," said he, in his serious way, inclining his large head towards one side and looking into her face with his dark, lifeless eyes.

His father and mother were pleased with this attitude of their daughter towards her brother. They praised her good heart in his presence and by degrees she became the acknowledged guardian of the hunchback. She taught him to play with toys, helped him to prepare his lessons, read him stories about princes and fairies.

But, as formerly, he piled his toys in tall heaps, as if trying to reach something. He did his lessons carelessly and badly; but at the marvellous in tales he smiled in a curious, indecisive way, and once he asked his sister:

"Are princes ever hunchbacks?"

"No."

"And knights?"

"Of course not."

The boy sighed, as though tired; but putting her hand on his bristly hair his sister said:

"But wise wizards are always hunchbacks."

"That means that I shall be a wizard," submissively remarked the hunchback, and then, after pondering a while, he said:

"Are fairies always beautiful?"

"Always."

"Like you?"

"Perhaps. I think they are even more beautiful," she said frankly.

When he was eight years old his sister noticed that when, during their walks, they passed houses in course of construction a strange expression of astonishment always appeared on the boy's face; he would look intently at the people working and then turn his expressionless eyes questioningly to her.

"Does that interest you?" she asked. And he, who spoke little as a rule, replied:

"Yes."

"Why?"

"I don't know."

But once he explained:

"Such little people, and such small bricks, and the houses are so big.... Is the whole town made like that?"

"Yes, of course."

"And our house?"

"Of course."

Looking at him she said in a decisive manner:

"You will be a famous architect, that's it."

They bought a lot of wooden cubes for him, and from that time on an ardent passion for building took possession of him: for whole days he would sit silently on the floor of his room, building tall towers, which fell down with a crash, only to be built again. So constant did his preoccupation become that even at table, during dinner, he used to try to build things with the knives and forks and napkin rings. His eyes became deeper and more concentrated, his arms more agile and very restless, and he handled every object that came within his reach.

Now, during their walks in the town, he was ready to stand for hours in front of a building in construction, observing how from a small thing it grew huge, rising towards the sky. His nostrils quivered as they took in the smell of the brick dust and lime. His eyes became clouded, as if covered with a film, and he seemed deeply engrossed in thought. When he was told that it was not the proper thing to stand in the street he did not hear.

"Let us go!" His sister would rouse him, taking his arm.

He lowered his head and walked on, but kept looking back over his shoulder.

"You will become an architect, won't you?" she asked him repeatedly, trying to inculcate this idea in him.

"Yes."

Once after dinner, while waiting for the coffee in the sitting-room, the father remarked that it was time for him to leave his toys and begin to study in real earnest, but the sister, speaking in a tone which indicated that her authority was recognised, and that her opinion too had to be reckoned with, said:

"I hope, papa, that you will not send him to school."

The father, who was tall, clean-shaven and adorned with a large number of sparkling precious stones, replied, lighting his cigar:

"Why not?"

"You know why."

As the conversation turned upon the hunchback he quietly walked out of the room; but he walked slowly and heard his sister say:

"They will jeer at him."

"Yes, of course," said the mother, in a low tone, which sounded as cheerless as the autumn wind.

"Boys such as he should be kept in the background," his sister said fervently.

"Yes, he is nothing to be proud of," said the mother. "There is not much sense in his little head."

"Perhaps you are right," the father agreed.

"No, there's a lot of sense."

The hunchback came back, stopped in the doorway and said:

"I am not a fool either."

"We shall see," said the father; and his mother remarked:

"No one thinks anything of the sort."

"You will study at home," declared his sister, making him sit down by her side.

"You will study everything that it is necessary for an architect to know. Would you like that?"

"Yes, you will see."

"What shall I see?"

"What I like."

She was slightly taller than he, about half a head, but she domineered over everybody, even her father and mother. At that time she was fifteen; he resembled a crab, but she was slim and straight and strong and seemed to him a fairy, under whose power the whole house lived—even he, the little hunchback.

Polite, formal people came to him, explaining things and putting questions to him. But he confessed frankly that he did not understand what they were trying to teach him, and would look in an absent-minded way past his instructors, preoccupied with his own thoughts. It was clear to everybody that he took no interest in ordinary things. He spoke little, but sometimes he asked strange questions.

"What happens to those who don't want to do anything at all?"

The well-trained tutor, in his tightly buttoned black frock-coat—he resembled at once a priest and a soldier—replied: "Everything bad happens to such people, anything that you can imagine. For instance, many of them become socialists."

"Thank you," said the hunchback. His attitude towards his teachers was always correct and reserved, like that of an adult. "And what is a socialist?" "At best he is a dreamer and a lazy fellow—a moral freak who is deprived of all idea of God, property and nationality."

The teachers always replied briefly and to the point. Their answers fixed themselves in one's memory as tightly as if they were the stones of a pavement.

"Can an old woman also be a moral freak?"

"Of course in their midst——"

"And girls too?"

"Yes, it is an inborn quality."

The teachers said of him:

"He has little capacity for mathematics, but he shows great interest in moral questions."

"You speak too much," said his sister to him on hearing of his talks with the tutors.

"They talk more than I do."

"You pray very little to God."

"He won't set my hump right."

"Oh, is that how you are beginning to think!" exclaimed his sister in astonishment; and she warned him:

"I will excuse you this time, but don't entertain such thoughts again. Do you hear?"

"Yes."

She already wore long dresses; he was then just thirteen.

And now a number of annoyances began to fall to her lot: almost every time she entered her brother's work-room, boards and tools and blocks of all sorts fell at her feet, grazing her shoulder, her head, or hurting her hands. The hunchback always cautioned her by a cry of:

"Look out!"

But he was always too slow and the damage was done. Once, limping slightly, pale and very angry, she sprang at him, and shouted in his face:

"You do all this purposely, you freak," and she struck him in the face.

His legs were weak, he fell down, and, as he sat on the floor, quietly, without tears and without complaining, he said to her:

"How can you think that? You love me, don't you? Do you love me?"

She ran away groaning. Presently she came back.

"You see this never happened formerly," she explained.

"Nor this," he quietly remarked, making a wide circle with his long hand: in the corners of the room boards and boxes were heaped up; everything was in confusion; there were piles of wood on the carpenter's and turner's benches which stood against the wall.

"Why have you brought in all this rubbish?" she asked, looking doubtfully and squeamishly around.

"You will see."

He had begun to build, he had made a little rabbit hutch and a dog kennel. He was planning a rat-trap. His sister followed his work with interest and at table spoke proudly to his mother and father about it. His father, nodding his head approvingly, said:

"Everything springs from small beginnings and everything begins like that."

And his mother, embracing her, said to her son:

"You don't realise how much you owe to her care of you."

"Yes, I do," replied the hunchback.

When he had finished the rat-trap he asked his sister into his room and showed her the clumsy contrivance, saying:

"This is not a toy, mind you, and we can take out a patent for it. See how simple and strong it is; touch it here."

The girl touched it; something snapped and she screamed wildly; but the hunchback, dancing around her, muttered:

"Oh, not that, not that."

His mother ran up, and the servants came; they broke the rat-trap, and freed the girl's finger, which had turned quite blue. They carried her away fainting, and the boy's mother said to him:

"I will have everything thrown away. I forbid you."

At night he was asked to go to his sister, who said to him:

"You did it purposely. You hate me. What for?"

Moving his hunch he said quietly and calmly:

"You touched it with the wrong hand."

"That's a lie."

"But why should I hurt your hand? It is not even the hand you hit me with."

"Look out, you freak, I'll pay you out."

"I know."

There were no signs that he pitied his sister or looked upon himself as being to blame for her misfortune. His angular face was as calm as it always was, the expression of his eyes was serious and steady—it was impossible to believe that he could lie or be actuated by malice.

After that she did not go so often to his room. She was visited by her friends, chattering girls in bright coloured dresses, as noisy as so many crickets. They brought a welcome note of colour and gaiety to the large rooms, which were rather cold and gloomy—the pictures, the statues, the flowers, the gilt, everything seemed warmer in their presence. Sometimes his sister took them to his room. They affectedly held out their little pink-nailed fingers, taking his hand gingerly as if they were afraid of breaking it. They talked to him very nicely and pleasantly, looking a little astonished, but showing no particular interest in the little hunchback, busy in the midst of tools, drawings, pieces of wood and shavings. He knew that the girls called him "the inventor." His sister had impressed this idea upon them and told them that in the future something might be expected of him which would make the name of his father famous. His sister spoke of this with conviction.

"Of course he is ugly, but he is very clever," she reminded them very often.

She was nineteen years old, and had a sweetheart, when her father and mother both perished at sea. The yacht in which they were taking a pleasure trip was run down and sunk by an American cargo boat in charge of a drunken helmsman. She was to have accompanied them, but a sudden toothache had prevented her going.

When the news came of her father's and mother's death she forgot her tooth-ache, and rushed about the room throwing up her arms and crying:

"No, no; it cannot be."

The hunchback stood at the door and, wrapping the portiere round him, looked at her closely and said, shaking his hunch:

"Father was so round and hollow; I don't see how he could be drowned."

"Be quiet; you do not love anybody!" shouted his sister.

"I simply cannot say nice words," he replied.

The father's corpse was never found, but the mother had been killed in the moment of the collision. Her body was recovered and laid in a coffin, looking as lean and brittle as the dead branch of an old tree—just as she had looked when she was alive.

"Now you and I are left alone," the sister said to her brother sternly, but in a mournful voice, after the mother's funeral; and the cold look in her grey eyes daunted him. "It will be hard for us: we are ignorant of the world and may lose much. What a pity it is that I cannot get married at once."

"Oh!" exclaimed the hunchback.

"What do you mean by 'Oh'?"

He said, after thinking a while:

"We are alone."

"You seem to speak as if you rejoiced at it."

"I do not rejoice at anything."

"What a pity it is you are so little like a man."

In the evenings her lover came—an active little man, with white eyebrows and eyelashes, and a round sunburnt face relieved by a woolly moustache. He laughed continuously the whole evening, and probably could have laughed the whole day long. They were already engaged, and a new house was being built for them in one of the best streets of the town, the cleanest and the quietest. The hunchback had never seen this building and did not like to hear others talk of it. One day the fiancé slapped him on the shoulder with his plump and much beringed little hand, and said, showing a great number of tiny teeth:

"You ought to come and look over it, eh? What do you say?"

He refused for a long time under different pretexts, but at last he gave way and went with him and his sister. The two men climbed to the top storey of the scaffolding and then fell. The fiancé dropped plump to the ground into the lime-pit, but the brother, whose clothes got caught in the scaffolding, hung in mid-air and was rescued by the workmen. He had no worse than a dislocated leg and wrist and a badly bruised face. The fiancé, on the other hand, broke his back and was severely gashed in the side.

The sister fell into convulsions, and tore at the ground with her hands, raising little clouds of white dust. She wept almost continuously for more than a month and then became like her mother. She grew thin and haggard, and began to speak in a cold, expressionless voice.

"You are my misfortune," she said.

He answered nothing, but kept his large eyes bent upon the ground. His sister dressed herself in black, made her eyebrows meet in a line, and whenever she met her brother clenched her teeth so that her jaw-bones made sharp angles. He, on his part, tried to avoid meeting her eye and was for ever busy planning and designing, alone in silence. So he lived till he was of age, and then began between them an open struggle to which their whole life was given, a struggle which bound them to each other by the strong links of mutual insults and offences.

On the day of his coming of age he said to her in the tone of an elder brother:

"There are no wise wizards, and no kind fairies. There are only men and women, some of them wicked, others stupid, and everything that is said about goodness is a myth. But I want the myth to become a reality. Do you remember saying, 'In a rich house everything should be beautiful and smart'? In a rich town also everything should be beautiful. I am buying some land outside the town and am going to build a house there for myself and for freaks like me. I shall take them out of the town, where their life is almost unendurable and where it is unpleasant for people like you to look upon them."

"No," she said; "you certainly will not do that. It is a crazy idea."

"It is your idea."

They disputed about it in the coldly hostile manner in which two people dispute who hate each other bitterly, and have no need to disguise their hatred.

"It is decided," he said.

"Not by me," his sister replied.

He raised his hunch and went off; and soon after his sister discovered that the land had been bought and, what was more, that workmen were already digging trenches for the foundation; that tens of thousands of bricks were being carted, and stones and iron and wood.

"Do you think you are still a boy?" she asked. "Do you think it is a game?"

He made no answer.

Once a week his sister, lean and straight and proud, drove into the town in her little carriage drawn by a white horse. She drove slowly past the spot where the work was proceeding and looked coldly at the red bricks, like little chunks of meat, held in place by a framework of iron girders; yellow wood was being fitted into the ponderous mass like a network of nerves. She saw in the distance her brother's crab-like figure. He crawled about the scaffolding, stick in hand, a crumpled hat upon his head. He was covered with dust and looked like a grey spider. At home she gazed intently at
86

his excited face and into his dark eyes, which had become softer and clearer.

"No," he said quietly to himself, "I have hit upon an idea: it should be equally good for all concerned! It is wonderful work to build, and it seems to me that I shall soon consider myself a happy man."

"Happy?" she asked wonderingly, measuring with her eyes the hunchback's body.

"Yes, you know people who work are quite unlike us, they awaken new thoughts in one.... How good it must be to be a bricklayer walking through the streets of a town where he has built dozens of houses. There are many socialists among the workers—steady, sober fellows, first of all. Truly they have their own sense of dignity.... Sometimes it seems to me that we don't understand our people."

"You are talking strangely," she said.

The hunchback was becoming animated, getting more and more talkative every day.

"In reality everything is turning out as you wished it: I am becoming a wise wizard who frees the town from freaks. You could be a good fairy if you wished. Why don't you help me?"

"We will speak about it later," she said, playing with her gold watch-chain.

Once he spoke out in a language quite unfamiliar to her:

"Maybe I have wronged you more than you have wronged me."

She was astonished.

"I wronged you?"

"Wait a minute. Upon my word of honour I am not as guilty as you think. I walk badly. I may have pushed him, but there was no malicious intention. No, believe me. I am more guilty of having wanted to injure your hand, the hand you hit me with."

"Don't let us speak about that," she said.

"It seems to me one ought to be kinder," muttered the hunchback. "I think that goodness is not a myth—it is possible."

The big building in the town grew rapidly; it had spread over the rich soil and was rising towards the sky, which was always grey, always threatening with rain.

Once a little group of officials came to the place where the work was proceeding. They examined the building and, after talking quietly among themselves, gave orders to stop the work.

"You have done this," exclaimed the hunchback, rushing at his sister and clutching her throat with his long, nervous hands; but some men ran up and pulled him away from her. The sister said to them:

"You see, gentlemen, he is really abnormal, and must be looked after. This sort of thing began immediately after the death of his father, whom he loved passionately. Ask the servants: they all know of his illness. They kept silence until latterly, these good people; the honour of the house where many of them have lived since their childhood is dear to them. I also tried to hide our misfortune. An insane brother is not a thing to be proud of."

His face turned purple and his eyes started out of their sockets as he listened to this speech. He was dumbfounded, and silently scratched with his nails the hands of those who held him while she continued:

"This house was a ruinous enterprise. I intend to give it to the town, in the name of my father, as an asylum for insane people."

He shrieked, lost consciousness and was carried away.

His sister continued the building with the same speed with which he had been conducting it, and when the house was finished, the first patient who went into it was her brother. Seven years he spent there—ample time for him to develop melancholia and become an imbecile. His sister turned old in the meantime. She lost all hope of ever becoming a mother, and when at last she saw that he was vanquished and would not rise against her she took him under her care.

And now they are travelling all over the globe, hither and thither, like blinded birds. They look on everything without sense or joy, and see nothing anywhere except themselves.

ON THE STEAMER

The blue water seems as thick as oil. The screw of the steamer works softly, almost silently. One can detect no trembling of the deck and the mast, pointing towards the clear sky, strains and quivers ever so slightly. The rigging, taut as the strings of an instrument, hums gently, but one has grown used to the vibration, and does not notice it, and it seems as if the steamer—white and graceful as a swan—were motionless on the smooth water. To perceive the motion one must look over the gunwale, where a greenish wave retreats from the white side of the steamer. It seems to fall away in broad soft folds, rolling and glistening like quicksilver and splashing dreamily.

It is morning. The sea seems half asleep. The rosy hues of sunrise have not yet disappeared from the sky. We have just passed the island of Gorgona, still slumbering. It is a stern, solitary rock, covered with woods and surmounted by a round grey tower; a cluster of little white houses can be seen at the edge of the sleepy water. A few small boats are moving rapidly on either side of the steamer, rowed by people from the island going to catch sardines. The measured splashing of the long oars and the slim figures of the fishermen linger in the memory. The men row standing and seem to be bowing to the sun.

Behind the ship's stern is a broad streak of greenish foam. Above it seagulls soar lazily. Now and then a bird seems to come from nowhere. It flies noiselessly, stretched out like a cigar, and, after skimming the surface of the water, suddenly darts into it like an arrow.

In the distance, like a cloud from the sea, rises the coast-line of Liguria, with its violet mountains. In another two or three hours the steamer will enter the narrow harbour of the marble town of Genoa.

The sun climbs higher and higher, promising a hot day.

The stewards run up on to the deck; one of them is young, thin, and quick in his movements, like a Neapolitan, with an ever-changing expression on his mobile face; the other is a man of medium height, with a grey moustache, black eyebrows, and silvery bristles on his round skull. He has an aquiline nose and serious, intelligent eyes. Laughing and joking they quickly lay the table for breakfast and depart. Then one after another the passengers creep slowly from their cabins. First comes a fat man with a small head and red bloated face; he looks melancholy and his tired swollen red lips are half open. He is followed by a tall, sleek man with grey side-whiskers, eyes that cannot be seen, and a little nose that looks like a button on his flat yellow face. After them, leaping over the brass rail of the companion-way, comes a plump red-haired man, with a moustache curled in military fashion; he is dressed like an Alpine mountaineer, and wears a green feather in his hat. All three stop near the gunwale. The fat man, half-closing his sad eyes, remarks:

"How calm it is!"

The man with the side-whiskers put his hands into his pockets, spread out his legs, and stood there resembling a pair of open scissors. The red-haired man took out his large gold watch, which looked like the pendulum of a clock, looked at it, then at the sky and along the deck; then he began to whistle, swinging his watch and beating time with his foot.

Two ladies came up, the younger, embonpoint, with a porcelain face and amiable milky-blue eyes. Her dark brows seemed to have been pencilled and one was higher than the other. The other was older, sharp-featured, and her headdress of faded hair looked enormous. She had a large black mole on her left cheek, two gold chains round her neck, and a lorgnon and a number of trinkets hanging from the belt of her grey dress.

Coffee was served; the young lady sat down silently at the table and began to pour out the black liquid, affectedly curving her arms, which were bare to the elbow.

The men came to the table and sat down in silence. The fat man took a cup and said sighing:

"It is going to be hot."

"You are spilling it on to your knees," remarked the elder lady.

He looked down, his chin and cheeks became puffed out as they rested on his chest; he put his cup on the table, wiped drops of coffee off his grey trousers with a handkerchief, and then wiped his face, which was in a perspiration.

"Yes," unexpectedly remarked the red-haired man in a loud voice, shuffling his short legs. "Yes, yes, even if the Parties of the Left have begun to complain about hooliganism it means— —"

"Don't chatter, John," interrupted the elder lady. "Isn't Lisa coming out?"

"She doesn't feel well," answered the younger lady in a sonorous voice.

"But the sea is quite calm."

"Oh, but when a woman is in her condition."

The red-haired man smiled voluptuously and closed his eyes.

Beyond the gunwale, breaking the calm expanse of the sea, porpoises were making a commotion. The man with the side-whiskers, watching them attentively, said:

"The porpoises look like pigs."

The red-haired man chimed in:

"There is plenty of piggery here."

The colourless lady raised a cup to her lips, smelt the coffee and made a grimace.

"It is disgusting."

"And the milk, eh?" said the fat man, blinking and seeming ill at
ease.

The lady with the porcelain face said in a sing-song voice:
"Everything is very dirty, and they all look very much like Jews."

The red-haired man was rapidly whispering something into the ear
of the man with the side-whiskers, as if he were giving replies to his
teacher, proud of having learnt his lesson well. His listener seemed
tickled, and betrayed curiosity. He wagged his head slightly from
side to side, and, in his fat face, his wide-open mouth looked like a
hole in a dried-up board. At times he seemed to want to say
something and began in a strange, hoarse voice:

"In our province— —"

But without continuing he again attentively inclined his head to the
lips of the red-haired man.

The fat man sighed heavily, saying:

"How you buzz, John!"

"Well, give me some coffee."

He drew up to the table, causing a clatter, and his companion said
impressively:

"John has ideas— —"

"You have not had enough sleep," said the elder lady, looking
through her lorgnon at the man with the side-whiskers. The latter
passed his hand over his face, then looked at his palm.

"I seem to have got some powder on my face. Do you notice it?"

"Oh, uncle," exclaimed the younger lady, "that is a peculiarity of
beautiful Italy! One's skin dries here so terribly!" The elder lady
inquired:

"Do you notice, Lydia, how bad the sugar is here?"

A man of large proportions came on deck. His grey, curly hair looked like a cap. He had a big nose, merry eyes and a cigar between his lips. The stewards who stood near the gunwale bowed reverently to him.

"Good-morning, boys, good-morning," said he, in a loud, hoarse voice, benevolently nodding his head.

The Russians became silent, looking askance at the new-comer from time to time. John of the military moustache said in a low voice:

"A retired military man, one can see at once——"

Noticing that he was being observed the grey-haired man took the cigar from his mouth and bowed pleasantly to the Russians. The elder lady threw back her head and, raising her lorgnon to her nose, looked at him defiantly. The man with the moustache was embarrassed and, turning away, took out his watch and began to swing it in the air. Only the fat man acknowledged the greeting, pressing his chin against his chest. The Italian became embarrassed in his turn. He pushed his cigar nervously into a corner of his mouth and asked the middle-aged steward in a low tone:

"Are those Russians?"

"Yes, sir: a Russian Governor and his family."

"What kind faces they always have." "Very nice people."

"The best of the Slavs of course."

"They are a trifle careless I should say."

"Careless? Why?"

"It seems so to me—they are careless in their treatment of people."

The fat Russian blushed and, smiling broadly, said in a subdued tone:

"They are speaking about us."

"What?" asked the elder lady, with a disdainful grimace.

"They are saying we are the best of the Slavs," answered the fat man, with a giggle.

"They are such flatterers," declared the lady, but red-haired John put away his watch and, twisting his moustache with both hands, said, in an off-hand way:

"They are all amazingly ignorant about everything that concerns us."

"You are being praised," said the fat man, "and you say it is due to ignorance." "Nonsense! That is not what I mean, but generally speaking.... I know myself that we are the best of Slavs."

The man with the side-whiskers, who for some time had been attentively watching the porpoises at play, sighed and, shaking his head, remarked:

"What a stupid fish!"

Two more persons joined the greyhaired Italian: an old bespectacled man in a black frock-coat and a pale youth with long hair, a high forehead and dark eyebrows. They all stood at the gunwale about five yards from the Russians; the grey-haired man said quietly:

"When I see Russians I think of Messina."

"Do you remember how we met the sailors at Naples?" asked the youth.

"Yes, they will never forget that day in their forests!"

"Have you seen the medal struck in their honour?"

"I do not think much of the workmanship."

"They are talking about Messina," the fat man informed his companions.

"And they laugh!" exclaimed the younger lady. "It is amazing!"

Seagulls overtook the steamer, and one of them, beating its crooked wings, seemed to hang in the air over the gunwale; the younger lady began to throw biscuits to it. The birds, in catching the pieces, disappeared below the gunwale and then, shrieking greedily, rose again in the blue void above the sea. Some coffee was brought to the Italians: they also began to feed the birds, tossing up pieces of biscuits. The lady raised her brows and said:

"Look at the monkeys."

The fat man continued to listen to the animated talk of the Italians and presently said:

"He is not a military man, he is a merchant. He talks about trading in corn with us, and about being able to buy petroleum, timber and coal from us."

"I noticed at once that he was not a military man," said the elder lady.

The red-haired man began again to speak into the ear of the man with side-whiskers. The latter screwed up his mouth sceptically as he listened to him. The young Italian, glancing sideways at the Russians, said:

"What a pity it is that we know so little about this country of big, blue-eyed people!"

The sun was now high in the sky and burning hotly; the sea glistened and dazzled one. In the distance, on the port side, mountains and clouds appeared out of the water.

"Annette," said the man with the side-whiskers, his smile reaching his ears, "just think what an idea has struck funny John! He has hit upon the best way of ridding the villages of malcontents. It is very ingenious."

And rolling in his chair he related in a slow and halting manner, as if he were translating from another language: "The idea is that on holidays and market-days the local 'district chief' should get together, at the public expense, a great quantity of stakes and stones; and should then set out before the peasants, also at the public expense, thirty, sixty, a hundred and fifty gallons of vodka, according to the number of people. That is all that is wanted!"

"I don't understand," declared the elder lady. "Is it a joke?"

The red-haired man answered quickly:

"No, it is quite serious. Just think of it, ma tante."

The younger lady opened her eyes wide, and shrugged her shoulders.

"What nonsense to let them drink Government vodka when they already.

"No, wait a bit, Lydia," exclaimed the red-haired man, jumping up from his chair. The man with the side-whiskers rocked from side to side, laughing noiselessly with his mouth wide open.

"Just think of it! The hooligans who don't succeed in getting dead drunk will kill one another with the sticks and stones. Don't you see?"

"Why one another?" asked the fat man.

"Is it a joke?" inquired the elder lady again.

The red-haired man waved his short arms excitedly and tried to explain.

"When the authorities pacify them, the Parties of the Left cry out about cruelty and atrocities. That means that a way must be found by which they can pacify themselves. Don't you agree?" The steamer gave a lurch and the crockery rattled. The plump lady was alarmed and caught hold of the table; and the elder lady, laying her hand on the fat man's shoulder, asked sharply:

"What's that?"

"We are turning."

The coast, rising out of the water, becomes higher and more defined. One can see the gardens on the slopes of the mist-enveloped hills and mountains. Bluish boulders peep out from among the vineyards; white houses appear through the haze. The window-panes glisten in the sun and patches of bright colour greet the eye. Right on the water's edge, at the foot of the cliffs, a little house faces the sea; it is overhung with a thick mass of bright violet flowers. Above it, pouring like a broad red stream over the stones of the terraces, is a profusion of red geraniums. The colours are gay, the coast-line looks amiable and hospitable. The soft contours of the mountains seem to entice one into the shade of the gardens.

"How small everything is here!" said the fat man, with a sigh. The elder lady looked at him sharply; then, compressing her thin lips and throwing back her head, gazed through her lorgnon at the coast.

A number of dark-complexioned people in light costumes are now on deck, talking loudly. The Russian ladies look at them disdainfully, as queens on their subjects.

"How they wave their arms," said the younger lady, and the fat man, catching his breath, explained:

"It is the fault of their language. It is poor and requires gestures."

"O Lord!" said the elder lady, with a deep sigh. Then after a pause she inquired:

"Are there many museums in Genoa?"

"I understand there are three," answered the fat man.

"And a cemetery?" asked the younger lady.

"Campo Santo? And churches, of course."

"Are the cabmen as bad as in Naples?" "As bad as in Moscow."

The red-haired man and the man with the side-whiskers rose and moved away from the gunwale, talking together earnestly and interrupting one another.

"What is the Italian saying?" asked the lady, adjusting her gorgeous headdress. Her elbows were pointed, her ears large and yellow, like faded leaves. The fat man listened attentively and obediently to the animated talk of the curly-headed Italian.

"It seems that there is a very old law which forbids the Jews to enter Moscow. It is no doubt a relic of former despotism, you know, of John the Terrible. Even in England there are many obsolete laws unrepealed even to this day. It may be that the Jew was trying to mislead me; anyhow, for some reason or other he was not allowed to enter Moscow, the ancient city of the Tsars, of sacred things."

"But here in Rome the Mayor is a Jew—in Rome, which is more ancient and more sacred than Moscow," said the youth, smiling.

"And he gives the Pope some very shrewd knocks—the little tailor. Let us wish him success in that," put in the old man in spectacles, clapping his hands.

"What is the old man saying?" asked the lady.

"Just a minute! Some nonsense. They speak the Neapolitan dialect."

"This Jew went to Moscow, however—they must have blood—and there he goes to the house of a prostitute. It was the only place he could go to, so he said."

"A fairy tale!" said the old man decisively; and he waved his arm as if brushing the tale aside.

"To tell you the truth, I am of the same opinion."

"Of course, it's a fable!"

"And what was the sequel?" asked the youth.

"He was betrayed by her to the police; but she took his money first."

"What baseness," said the old man. "He is a man with a dirty imagination, that's all. I know some Russians who were with me at the University; they are fine fellows."

"But listen to me. The strange thing was ..."

"I have heard it said ..."

The fat Russian, wiping his perspiring face with a handkerchief, said to the ladies in an idle, indifferent tone:

"He is telling a Jewish anecdote."

"With such animation?" smiled the young lady; and the other remarked:

"In these people, with their gestures and their noise, there is a lack of variety." A town grows on the coast, houses rise from beyond the hills and huddle close together, until they form a solid wall of buildings which reflect the sunlight and look as if they were carved out of ivory.

"It is like Yalta," remarked the young lady, rising up. "I will go to Lisa."

She ambled her portly body, which was clothed in some bluish material, slowly along the deck. As she passed the group of Italians the grey-haired man interrupted his speech and said quietly:

"What fine eyes!"

"Yes," nodded the old man in spectacles. "Basilida, I imagine, must have looked like that."

"Basilida, the Byzantine?"

"I picture her as a Slav woman."

"They are saying something about Lydia," said the fat man.

"What?" asked the lady. "No doubt some low jokes?"

"About her eyes. They admire— —"

The lady made a grimace.

The brasswork on the steamer glistened as, gently and rapidly, she neared the shore. The black walls of the pier came in sight and, beyond them, rising into the sky, a forest of masts. Here and there bright coloured flags hung motionless; dark smoke ascended and seemed to melt in the air; there was a smell of oil and coal dust; the noise of work proceeding in the harbour and the complex bourdon note of a large town reached the ear.

The fat man suddenly burst out laughing.

"What's the matter?" asked the lady, half-closing her grey, faded eyes.

"The Germans will smash them up, by Jove! You will see it!"

"Why should you rejoice at that?"

"Just so."

The man with the side-whiskers, examining the soles of his boots, asked the red-haired man, speaking deliberately and in a loud voice:

"Were you satisfied with this surprise or not?"

The red-haired man twisted his moustache fiercely, and made no reply.

The steamer slowed down. The green water splashed against the white sides of the ship, as if in protest. It gave no reflection of the marble houses, the high towers and the azure terraces. The black jaws of the harbour opened, disclosing a thick scattering of ships.

THE PROFESSOR

The young man was ugly, and knew it. But he said to himself:

"I am clever, am I not? I will become a sage. It is an easy matter here in Russia."

He began to read bulky works, for he was by no means stupid: he understood that the presence of wisdom can most easily be proved by quotations from books.

Having read as many wise books as were necessary to make him short-sighted, he proudly held up his nose, which had become red from the weight of the spectacles, and declared to the world at large:

"Well, you won't deceive me. I see that life is a trap, put here for me by nature."

"And love?" asked the Spirit of Life.

"No, I thank you. Praise be to God, I am not a poet. I will not enter the iron cage of inevitable duties for the sake of a piece of cheese."

But he was only moderately talented, and so he decided to take up the duties of a professor of philosophy.

He went to the Minister of Popular Education and said to him:

"Your Excellency, I can preach that life is meaningless, and that one should not submit to the dictates of nature."

The Minister considered a while whether that would do, then asked:

"Should the orders of the authorities be obeyed?"

"Most decidedly," said the philosopher, reverently inclining his head, which the study of so many books had rendered bald. "Since human passions— —"

"Very well, you may have the chair. Your salary will be sixteen roubles a month. But should I require you to take into consideration the laws of nature, take care, have no opinions of your own. I shall not put up with that."

After thinking for some moments the Minister added, in a melancholy voice: "We live at a time when, for the sake of the unity of the state, it will perhaps be necessary to recognise that the laws of nature not only exist, but that they may to a certain extent prove useful."

"Just think of it!" exclaimed the philosopher to himself. "Even I may live to see it." But aloud he said nothing.

So he settled down to his work: every week he ascended the rostrum and spoke for an hour to curly-headed youths in this strain:

"Gentlemen, man is limited from without, he is limited from within. Nature is antagonistic to him. Woman is a blind tool of Nature. All our life, therefore, is meaningless."

He had grown accustomed to think like this himself, and often in his enthusiasm he spoke eloquently and well. The young students were enthusiastic in their applause. He, pleased with himself, nodded his bald head and smiled at them kindly. His little nose shone, and everything went on smoothly.

Dining at a restaurant disagreed with him—like all pessimists he suffered from indigestion—so he got married and ate his dinners at home for twenty-nine years. In between his work—he had not noticed how—he brought up four children. Then he died.

Behind his coffin solemnly walked his three grief-stricken daughters with their young husbands, and his son, a poet, who was in love with all the beautiful women in the world. The students sang: "Eternal Memory." They sang loudly and with animation, but badly. Over his grave his colleagues, the professors, made flowery speeches, referring to the well-ordered metaphysics of the departed; everything was done in correct style; it was solemn, and at times even touching.

"Well, the old man is dead," said a student to his comrades as they were leaving the cemetery.

"He was a pessimist," chimed in another.

A third one asked:

"Is that so?"

"Yes, a pessimist and a conservative." "What, the bald-headed one was? I had not noticed it."

The fourth student was a poor man, and he inquired expectantly:

"Shall we be invited to the obituary feast?"

Yes, they had been invited.

During his lifetime the deceased had written a number of excellent books, in which he proved, in glowing and beautiful language, the vanity of life. Needless to say, the books were bought and read with pleasure. Whatever may be said to the contrary, man likes what is beautiful.

His family was well provided for—even pessimism can achieve that.

The obituary feast was arranged on a large scale. The poor student had a good meal, such as he seldom had, and as he went home he thought, smiling good-humouredly:

"Well, even pessimism is useful at times."

THE POET

There was another case.

A man, thinking himself a poet, wrote verse. But for some reason it was poor verse, and the circumstance disconcerted him.

Walking in the street one day, he saw a whip lying in the road, lost by a cabman. An inspiration came to the poet, and the following image at once formed itself in his mind:—

> "In the road, in the dust, the snake lies,
> Like a whip in the dust of the road.
> In a swarm, like a cloud, come the flies,
> And the ants and their kind in a swarm.
>
> Thro' the skin, like the links of a chain,
> Show the ribs—they show white thro' the skin.
> O dead snake, thou remind'st me again
> Of my love, my dead love, O dead snake."

Suddenly the whip stood up on end and, swaying, said to him:

"Why are you telling lies? You are a married man, you know how to read and write, yet you are telling lies. Your love has not died. You love your wife and you are afraid of her."

The poet became angry.

"That is no business of yours."

"And the verses are poor."

"They are better than you could make. You can only crack, and even that you cannot do by yourself."

"But, anyhow, why do you tell lies? Your love did not die."

"All kinds of things happen—it was necessary it should."

"Oh, your wife will whip you. Take me to her."

"Oh, you may wait."

"Well, well, go your own way," said the whip, curling itself up like a corkscrew; it lay down in the road and began to think of other people. The poet went to an inn, ordered a bottle of beer, and began to think about himself.

"Although the whip was decidedly rude, the verse is poor again, that's true enough. How strange it is! One person always writes bad verse, while another sometimes succeeds in writing verse that is good. How badly everything is arranged in this world! What a stupid world it is!"

So he sat and drank, trying to arrive at a clearer conception of the world. He came to the conclusion at last that it was necessary to speak the truth. This world is good for nothing, and it really disgusts a man to live in it. He thought about an hour and a half in this strain, and then he wrote:

> "For all their pleasant seeming, our desires
> A dread scourge are that drives us to our doom;
> Blindly we blunder thro' the maze where waits us
> Death, the fell serpent, in the murky gloom.
>
> Oh! let us strangle our insensate longings!
> They do but lure us from the appointed way;
> Lead us thro' thorns to our most bitter ruing,
> Leave us heartbroken in the twilight grey.
>
> And in the end full surely Death awaits us,
> Lives there the man but knows that he must die?"

He wrote more in the same spirit—twenty-eight lines in all.

"That's good!" exclaimed the poet; and went home quite satisfied with himself.

At home he read the lines to his wife. She liked them. She merely said:

"There is something wrong with the first four lines."

"They will swallow it all right. Pushkin too began rather badly. But what do you think of the metre? It is that of a requiem."

Then he began to play with his little son: he put him on his knee and, tossing him up, sang in a poor tenor:

> "Tramp, tramp,
> On somebody's bridge!
> When I grow rich
> I will pave my own bridge,
> And nobody else
> Shall walk over my bridge."

They spent the evening merrily, and the next morning the poet took his verses to an editor, who spoke in a profound manner (these editors are all profound—that is why their magazines are so dry)?

"H'm!" said the editor, rubbing his nose. "You know, this is not altogether bad, and, what is more important, it is quite in the spirit of the times. Very much so. You seem to have discovered yourself. You must continue in the same strain. Sixteen copecks a line ... four ... forty-eight. I congratulate you."

The verses were printed, and the poet felt as if he had had another birthday. His wife kissed him fervently, and said dreamily:

"Oh, my poet!"

They had a great time. But a youth, a very good youth, who was earnestly seeking the meaning of life, read these verses and shot himself dead.

He was quite convinced, you see, that, before denouncing life, the poet had sought the meaning as long as he himself had done, and that the search had been attended by sorrow, as in his own case.

The youth did not know that these sombre thoughts were sold at the rate of sixteen copecks a line. He was an earnest youth.

Let not the reader think I mean that even a whip can, at times, be used on people to their advantage.

THE WRITER

There once lived a very ambitious writer.

When he was abused, it seemed to him that he was abused too much, and unjustly. When he was praised he thought that they neither praised him enough, nor wisely. He lived in a state of perpetual discontent, until the time came for him to die.

The writer lay down on his bed and began grumbling:

"That's just how it is. What do you think of it? Two novels are not yet finished—and altogether I have enough material for ten years. The devil take this law of nature, and every other law. What nonsense! The novels might have turned out well. Why have they invented this idiotic compulsory service, as if things could not have been arranged differently? And it always comes at the wrong time: the novels are not finished yet."

He was angry, but disease was eating into his bones and whispering into his ears:

"You trembled, eh? Why did you tremble? You don't sleep at night, eh? Why don't you sleep? You have drunk of sorrow, eh?—and of joy too?"

He kept knitting his brows, but realised at last that nothing could be done. With a wave of the arm he dismissed the thought of his novels, and died.

It was very disagreeable, but he died.

So far so good. They washed him, dressed him according to custom, combed his hair and placed him on the table, straight and stiff like a soldier, heels together, toes apart. He lay very still, his nose drooped, and the only feeling he had was surprise.

"How strange it is that I feel nothing at all! It's the first time in my life. Ah, my wife is crying. Well, now you cry, but before, when anything went wrong, you flew into a rage. My little son is crying too. No doubt he will grow up a good-for-nothing fellow—the sons of writers, I have noticed, always do. No doubt that also is in accordance with some law of nature. What an infernal number of such laws there are."

So he lay and thought and thought, and wondered at his composure. He was not accustomed to it.

They started for the cemetery, but as he was being borne along he suddenly felt there were not enough mourners.

"No matter," said he to himself, "though I may not be a very great writer, literature must be respected."

He looked out of the coffin and saw that, as a matter of fact, without counting his relations, only nine people accompanied him, among whom were two beggars and a lamplighter with a ladder over his shoulder.

At this discovery he became quite indignant.

"What swine!"

The slight so incensed him that he immediately became resurrected, and, being a small man, jumped unperceived out of his coffin. He ran into a barber's, had his moustache and beard shaved off, and borrowed a black coat with a patch under the armpit, leaving his own coat in its stead. Then he made his face look solemn and aggrieved, and became like a living man. It was impossible to recognise him.

With the curiosity natural to his profession he asked the barber:

"Are you not astonished at this strange incident?"

The latter stroked his moustache condescendingly and replied:

"Well, we live in Russia, and we are used to all kinds of things."

"But then I am a deceased person and suddenly I change my attire?"

"It is the fashion of the times. And in what way are you a deceased person? Only externally! As far as the general run of people goes it would be better if God made them all like you. At the present time living people don't look half so natural."

"Don't I look rather yellowish?"

"Quite in the spirit of the epoch, as you should be. It is Russia—everyone here suffers from one ill or another."

It is well known that barbers are flatterers of the first order and the most obliging people on earth.

He bade him good-bye, and ran to overtake the coffin, moved by a keen desire to show for the last time his reverence for literature. He caught up with the procession and the number of those who accompanied the coffin became ten. The respect for the writer increased correspondingly. Passers-by exclaimed, astonished:

"Just look! A writer's funeral! Oh! Oh!"

And people who knew what was taking place thought, with a sort of pride, as they went about their business:

"It is plain that the importance of literature is being understood better and better by the country."

The writer was now following his own coffin as if he were an admirer of literature and a friend of the deceased. He addressed the lamplighter.

"Did you know the deceased person?"

"Certainly; I made use of him in a small way."

"I am very pleased to hear it."

"Yes; our work is like that of the sparrow; where something drops we pick it up."

"How am I to understand that?"

"Take it in a very simple manner, sir."

"In a simple manner?"

"Yes, certainly. Of course, it is a sin if one looks at it from a certain point of view. One cannot, however, get on in this world without using ones wits."

"H'm! Are you sure of that?"

"Quite sure, sir. There was a lamp right against his window, and every night he sat up till sunrise. Well, I did not light that lamp because enough light streamed from his window. So this one lamp was a net profit to me: he was a very useful man."

So, talking quietly to this one and that, the writer reached the cemetery, and it came to pass that he had to make a speech about himself, because all those who accompanied him on that day had toothache. This happened in Russia, and there people always have an ache of one sort or another.

He made a rather good speech. One paper went so far as to praise it in the following terms:—

"One of the followers, who from his appearance we judged to be an actor, made a warm and touching oration over the grave, albeit from our point of view he no doubt over-estimated and exaggerated the rather modest merits of the deceased. He was a writer of the old school who made no effort to rid himself of its defects—the naïve didactism, namely, and the over-insistence on the so-called civic duties—which to us nowadays have become so tiresome. Nevertheless, the speech was delivered with a feeling of unquestionable love for the written word." When the speech had been duly made the writer lay down in the coffin and thought, quite satisfied with himself:

"There, we are ready now. Everything has gone well and with dignity."

At this point he became quite dead. Thus should one's calling be respected, even though it be literature.

THE MAN WITH A NATIONAL FACE

Once upon a time there was a gentleman who had lived more than half his life, when he suddenly felt that something was lacking in him. He was very much alarmed.

He felt himself; everything seemed to be all right and in its place, his stomach was even protruding. He examined himself in a looking-glass, and saw that he had eyes, ears, and everything else that a serious man should have. He counted his fingers: there were ten right enough, and ten toes on his feet; but still he had an uncomfortable feeling that something was missing.

He was sadly puzzled.

He asked his wife:

"What do you think, Mitrodora? Is everything about me in order?"

She answered reassuringly:

"Everything."

"But sometimes it seems to me——"

She was a religious woman and advised him:

"Whenever you begin to imagine anything, recite mentally: 'Let God arise and his enemies will fall.'"

He questioned his friends also, in a roundabout way. They answered evasively, but looked at him suspiciously, as though he merited strong condemnation.

"What can it be?" thought the gentleman, feeling downcast.

He tried to recall his past. Everything seemed to be quite normal. He had been a socialist, had incited youths to revolt; but later on he had renounced everything, and for a long time now had strenuously trampled underfoot the "crops" himself had sown. Generally speaking he had lived like everybody else, in accordance with the spirit and inspirations of the times.

He pondered and pondered and suddenly discovered what it was:

"O Lord, I haven't got a national face!"

He rushed to the looking-glass and saw that his face really had an indistinct expression, like that of a blind man. It suggested a page of a translation from some foreign language, done carelessly by a more or less illiterate person who had omitted all punctuation, so that it was impossible to make out what was on the page. It might be read as containing either a demand that one's soul should be sacrificed for the liberty of the people, or that it was necessary to recognise the full sway of absolutism.

"H'm, what a mixture, to be sure," thought the gentleman; and he decided at once: "No, it is not the thing to live with a face like that."

So he began to wash it every day with expensive soaps, but this did not help: the skin shone, but the indistinctness remained. He began to lick his face with his tongue—his tongue was long and well adjusted, for at one time the gentleman had been engaged in journalism. But even his tongue was of no avail. He applied Japanese massage to his face, and bumps appeared, as they do after a hard fight, but still he could obtain no definiteness of expression.

He tried and tried, but without success; all that he achieved was to lose a pound and a half in weight. Suddenly to his joy he learned that the head constable of his district, von Judenfresser, was known for his understanding of national problems. He went to him and said:

"Matters stand so-and-so, your Honour. Cannot you help me in my trouble?"

The head constable of course was flattered: here was an educated man, not long since suspected of disloyalty to the throne, now asking advice with confidence on how to change the expression of his face. The constable chuckled, and in his great joy exclaimed:

"There is nothing simpler, my dear friend, my American gem. Rub your face against members of a subject nationality. Your real face will at once be revealed."

The gentleman was pleased, the weight of a mountain fell from his shoulders. He sniggered loyally and said to himself in some astonishment:

"Why could I not have guessed it myself? The whole matter is so simple."

They parted very good friends. The gentleman rushed out into the street, planted himself at a comer and waited. Presently a Jew came along; he rushed up to him and began:

"If you," he said, "are a Jew, you must become a Russian. If you do not want to, then— —"

The Jew (as is known from all anecdotes) belongs to a nervous and timid people. But this one was of a capricious character and would not put up with pogroms. He raised his arm, gave the gentleman a blow on the left cheek, and went home to his family.

The gentleman leaned against the wall, rubbing his face, and thinking:

"Well, well, the formation of one's national face is connected with sensations not always altogether agreeable, but let it be. Nekrassoff, although he was a poor poet, said quite truly:

> "Nothing can be got for naught:
> Fate demands its victims."

Suddenly a native of the Caucasus passed by. As proved by all anecdotes they are an uncivilised and hot-headed people. He was singing as he walked along:

118

"Mitskhales sakles mingrule."[1]

The gentleman pounced upon him:

"No," he said, "be quiet. If you are a Georgian you must become a Russian, and you must not love the hut of a Mingrelian, but what you are ordered to love. You must like prison, even without orders— —"

The Georgian left the gentleman in a horizontal position and went and drank Kachetin wine. The gentleman lay on the ground and pondered:

"Well, well, there are also Tartars, Armenians, Bashkirs, Kirghises, Mordva, Lithuanians. O Lord, what a number! And these are not all. There are our own people, the Slavs."

At this juncture a Little Russian came along, and of course he was singing in a very disloyal manner:

> "Our ancestors once led
> A happy life in Ukraina...."

"No," said the gentleman, rising to his feet. "Will you be kind enough in future to use the letter 'y' instead of 'oo';[2] otherwise you undermine the unity of the empire."

He argued the point at some length, and the Little Russian listened, for, as proved most conclusively by all the collections of Little Russian anecdotes, the Little Russians are a very slow people, and like to do their work without hurrying. Unfortunately this gentleman was somewhat insistent.

Some kind people picked the gentleman up and asked him:

"Where do you live?"

---

[1] "Love a Mingrelian hut."—Trans.

[2] The Little Russians speak a dialect of the language in which the Russian sound for "y" is pronounced "oo."

"In Great Russia."

Of course they took him to the police station. As they were driving along he felt his face, not without pride, though with a certain sense of pain. It seemed to him that it had grown considerably broader and he thought to himself:

"I believe I have acquired ..."

He was taken before von Judenfresser, and the latter, like the humane person he was, sent for the police doctor. When the doctor came they began to whisper to each other in surprise, and kept giggling, which seemed a strange thing to do in the circumstances.

"It is the first case in the whole of my practice," whispered the doctor. "I cannot make it out."

"What may that mean?" thought the gentleman, and asked:

"Well, how do I look?"

"The old face is quite rubbed off," answered von Judenfresser.

"And generally speaking has my face changed?"

"Of course it has, only, you know — —"

The doctor said consolingly:

"Your face is such, dear sir, that you may just as well put your trousers on it."

So it remained for the rest of his life. There is no moral here.

THE LIBERAL

There once lived a nobleman who liked to back up his statements by quoting history. Whenever he wanted to tell a lie, he went to a likely man and gave him the order:

"Egorka,[3] go and find me facts from history to prove that such-and-such a thing does not repeat itself, and vice versa."

Egorka was a smart fellow, and readily found what was wanted. The nobleman armed himself with these facts as occasion required and contrived to prove everything that was necessary. In fact, he was invincible.

He was, moreover, a plotter against the Government. At one time everyone thought it necessary to conspire against the Government. They were not afraid even to say to one another:

"The English have habeas corpus, but we have ukases."

And they made mock at these differences between nations.

Having done that, they would forget the Government oppression under which they suffered, and sit down and play whist till the cocks crew for the third time.

When the cocks announced the approach of mom the nobleman commanded:

"Egorka, sing something inspiring, and suitable to the hour."

Egorka stood up and, lifting his finger, reminded them in a manner full of meaning:

"In Holy Russia the cocks crow,

---

[3] By Egorka is meant the ordinary type of the Russian "intellectual" who has no backbone or principle, and is always at the beck and call of the landed proprietor, capitalist or the authorities.

It will soon be day in Holy Russia."

"Quite true," said the nobleman; "it will soon be day."

And they retired to rest.

So far so good; but suddenly the people began to get agitated. The nobleman noticed this and asked:

"Egorka, why are the people restless?"

The latter looked pleased as he reported:

"The people want to live like human beings."

"Well, who taught them that? I did. For fifty years I and my ancestors have fostered in them the idea that it was time for them to live like human beings; haven't we?"

He began to get excited and pressed Egorka eagerly.

"Find me facts from history about the agrarian movement in Europe. Texts from the Gospels about equality, and from the history of civilisation about the origin of property. Be quick about it."

Egorka was pleased. He perspired freely as he hurried hither and thither. He tore all the leaves out of the books, so that only the bindings were left. He carried big bundles of all kinds of convincing proofs to the nobleman, who still kept urging him on.

"Stick to it! When we have a constitution I will make you editor of a large Liberal paper."

And becoming quite bold at last he began himself to speak to the more moderate of the peasants.

"Besides," said he, "there were the brothers Gracchus in Rome; then in England, in Germany, in France.... And all this is historically necessary. Egorka, get me facts."

Thereupon he proved, by facts, that every nation is bound to desire liberty, even against the wish of the authorities.

The peasants of course were pleased and cried:

"We thank you humbly."

Everything went very well, harmoniously, in Christian love and mutual confidence, till suddenly the peasants began to ask:

"When are you going to clear out?"

"Clear out? Where?"

"Away."

"Where from?"

"Off the land."

And they laughed, saying:

"What a funny fellow. He understands everything, but he has ceased to understand what is simplest of all." They laughed, but the nobleman became angry.

"But listen to me," he said. "Why should I go if the land is mine?"

But the peasants did not heed him.

"How can it be yours when you have said yourself that it is the Lord's, and that even before the time of Jesus Christ there were some just men who knew it?" He did not understand them, and they did not understand him. So he went again to Egorka.

"Egorka, look up the ancient histories and find me ..."

But the latter replied in a perfectly independent spirit:

"All the histories were pulled to pieces to prove the contrary."

"You are lying, you plotter."

He rushed to the library and saw that it was true. Only the empty covers of the books remained. The surprise was so great that it threw him into a perspiration, and he began to appeal to his ancestors, saying sorrowfully:

"And who taught you to write history in such a one-sided manner? Look what you have done. Alas! what kind of history is it? To the devil with it!" But the peasants kept repeating the same thing:

"You have proved it all to us very clearly," they said. "Get away as quickly as you can, or else we shall drive you away."

Egorka had gone completely over to the peasants. When he met the nobleman he turned up his nose and laughed sneeringly:

"O you Liberal! Habeas corpus!"

Things went from bad to worse. The peasants sang songs and were in such high spirits that they carried off to their homes a stack of the nobleman's hay.

Suddenly the nobleman remembered that he had another card to play. In the entresol sat his great-grandmother, awaiting an inevitable death. She was so old that she had forgotten all human words; she could only remember one thing:

"Don't give ..."

Since the year 1861[4] she had not been able to say anything else.

He hastened to her, his feelings greatly agitated. He fell at her feet affectionately and appealed to her:

"Mother of mothers, you are a living history...."

But she only mumbled:

"Don't give..

———————————————————

[4] The year in which the serfs were liberated.

"But what is to be done?"

"Don't give..."

"But they want to drown me—to plunder me."

"Don't give..."

"But should I give full play to my desire not to let the Governor know?"

"Don't give..."

He obeyed the voice of this living history, and sent in the name of his greatgrandmother a telegram containing an irresistible appeal. Then he went out to the peasants and informed them:

"You have so frightened the old lady that she has sent for the soldiers. Be calm, nothing will happen, I shall not let the soldiers harm you."

Fierce-looking warriors galloped up on horseback. It was winter-time, and the horses, which had sweated freely on the way, began to shiver as the hoar-frost settled on them. The nobleman pitied the horses and stabled them on his estate, saying to the peasants:

"You carted away some hay to which you had no right; please send it back for these horses. They are animals, guilty of nothing; don't you understand?"

The soldiers were hungry; they caught and ate all the cocks in the village, and everything became peaceful in the nobleman's district. Egorka, of course, went over to the nobleman's side and, as before, the nobleman used his services in matters of history: he bought new copies of all the books and ordered all those facts to be erased which are apt to incline one towards Liberalism; and into those which could not be erased he ordered new sense to be put.

As for Egorka, he was equal to anything. To prove his versatility he turned his hand to pornography. Nevertheless a bright spot remained in his soul, and while he was busy blotting out historical facts his heart misgave him, and to appease his conscience he wrote verses and printed them under the nom de plume, "V. W."—i.e. "Vanquished Warrior."

> "O chanticler, thou harbinger of morn,
> How comes it that thy proud call has been stilled?
> How comes it that thy place of t'other day
> By yonder gloomy barn-owl now is filled?
> The nobleman he needs no future now,
> And all of us live each day like the last;
> Poor chanticler has long since ceased to crow
> And giv'n his drumsticks to a last repast.
> When shall we waken unto life once more?
> And who will call us when the dawn is nigh?
> If chanticler, poor chanticler, is dead,
> Pray who will wake and turn us out of bed?"

And the peasants of course calmed down; they now live in peace, and, as they have nothing else to do, spend their time making ribald verse:

> "O honest Mother!
> The Spring is nigh
> When we shall groan
> And, starving, die!"

The Russians are a happy people.

THE JEWS AND THEIR FRIENDS

Once upon a time, in a certain country, lived some Jews. They were ordinary Jews, fit for pogroms, for being slandered, or any other state requirements.

For example.

Whenever the native population began to show signs of being dissatisfied with life, the authorities removed certain clauses from the state regulations and sounded the following hope-awakening call:

"Draw near, you people; approach the seat of power."

The people drew near; and the authorities began to remonstrate with them:

"What is the cause of the agitation?"

"Your Honours, we have nothing to eat."

"Have you any teeth left?"

"Yes, a few."

"You see, you always manage to conceal something from the authorities."

When the local authorities found that the agitation could be suppressed by knocking out the remaining teeth, they immediately resorted to that remedy. But if they saw that harmonious relations could not be established by this means they began to ask tempting questions:

"What do you want?"

"Some land."

Some of them who were so deep sunken in ignorance that they were not able to understand what was in the interest of the state, went further and kept repeating:

"We want reforms of some kind in order that our teeth and ribs and insides, at least, may be regarded as our own property, and not be touched without cause."

The authorities reasoned with them:

"Oh, friends, why should you have these idle dreams? It is said that man liveth not by bread alone, also that one person that has been beaten is worth two that have not."

"And do they agree?"

"Who?"

"Those who have not been beaten?"

"Of course, dear friends. Did not the English ask us not very many years ago: 'Exile,' they said, 'all your own people to Siberia, and put us in their place. We,' they said, 'will pay the taxes punctually, and will drink twelve gallons of vodka per person per year, and, generally speaking..' 'No,' we said, 'why should we? Our people are all right, they are humble and obedient, they are not going to give us any trouble.' So now, you good fellows, instead of getting excited like this, don't you think you had better go and shake up the Jews a bit? What do you say to that? What else are they for?"

The people pondered and pondered; they saw that they could get no redress, so they decided to act upon the suggestion of the authorities.

"Well, fellows," they said, "with God's blessing we will smash them."

They ransacked fifty houses and killed a few Jews. But they soon tired of their labours, and, their desire for reforms being satisfied, everything went on as before.

Besides the authorities, the native population and the Jews, there lived some kind-hearted people in the state. Their function was to divert agitation into other channels and to quiet passions. After each pogrom their whole number came together, eighteen men in all, and sent forth to the world their written protest, thus:

"Although we know the Jews are Russian subjects, we are nevertheless convinced that they ought not to be utterly exterminated, and, therefore, taking all considerations into account, we hereby express our condemnation of this extreme persecution of living people. (Signed) High-Brow, Narrow-Chin, Long-Hair, Biting-Lip, Yea and Nay, Big Bellows, Joseph Three-Ear, Noisy-One, Know-All, Cyril Just-So, Flow-of-Words, Look-Wise, Quill-Driver, Lieutenant-Colonel (retired) Drink-no-Beer, Narym (solicitor), Busybody, On-All-Fours and Grisha In-the-Future, seven years old, a boy."

These protests appeared after each pogrom with the only difference that the age of Grisha kept changing and that Quill-Driver signed on behalf of Narym,[5] who was suddenly exiled to a town bearing the same name.

Sometimes the provinces responded to these protests:

"We sympathise and add our signatures," Pull-Apart telegraphed from Sleepy-Town, and Featherbrain from Daft Town; Samogryzoff "and others" from Okuroff also joined in. It was clear to everybody that "the others" were an invention, to make the message look more formidable, for there were no others in Okuroff.

The Jews were greatly distressed when they read these protests, and on one occasion one of them, who was a very shrewd man, made the following proposal:—

"Do you know what? You don't? Well, let us hide all the pens and ink and paper before the next pogrom, and see what these eighteen people, including Grisha, will do then."

---

[5] A well-known place of exile in Siberia.

These Jews knew how to act together. Once decided, they bought up and hid all the paper and pens and poured all the ink into the Black Sea. Then they quietly awaited the result.

They had not long to wait: the necessary permission was received from the authorities, a pogrom took place, the hospitals were full of Jews—and the humanitarians were running about St Petersburg looking for pens and paper. They could find none anywhere except in the offices of the authorities. And the latter would not give them any.

"What do you take us for?" they said. "We know what you want it for. No, you must do without it this time."

"But how can we?" Mr Busybody entreated them.

"Well," they answered, "you ought to realise by now that we have given you plenty of chances to protest."

Grisha, who was already forty-three years old, cried:

"I want to protest."

But there was nothing to protest on. A happy thought struck Know-All:

"Shall we write something on the fence at least?"

There were no fences in St Petersburg, only iron railings.

But they proceeded to the outskirts of the town, where, near the slaughterhouses, they came upon an old fence. No sooner, however, had Mr High-Brow made the first letter in chalk than, suddenly, as if dropping from the skies came a policeman and began to expostulate with him:

"What does this mean? When boys do this sort of thing they are whipped, but you, staid gentlemen, what are you doing?"

Of course he could not understand them, taking them for writers old enough to be writing their thousand and first article. They were nonplussed, and, scattering literally in all directions, went home.

So that one pogrom was not protested against, and the humanitarians were deprived of a pleasure.

People who understand the psychology of races say rightly: "The Jews are a shrewd people."

HARD TO PLEASE

Tired of their struggle with those who had opinions of their own, the authorities, wishing at last to rest on their laurels, once issued the following stringent order:—

"Hereby you are commanded to drag out into the light of day all those who have opinions of their own, to drag them out unceremoniously from their hiding-places, and to exterminate them by any measures that may seem necessary."

The execution of this order was entrusted to Oronty Strevenko, who had volunteered to exterminate living human beings of both sexes and of all ages. He was an ex-captain in the service of his Highness the King of the Fuegians, and an important personage in Terra del Fuego. For his services Oronty was allowed sixteen thousand roubles.

Oronty obtained the commission not because others could not be found as base, but because he looked unnaturally fierce, and was covered with an abundant growth of hair, which enabled him to go naked in all climates. Besides, he had four rows of teeth, sixty-four in all, a circumstance that won for him the special confidence of the authorities.

But in spite of all these advantages even he was confronted by the thought:

"How are they to be unearthed? They keep so quiet."

And in truth the inhabitants of this town were remarkably well trained. They went in fear of one another, seeing in everyone an agent-provocateur, and never asserted anything. Even in their talks with their mothers they spoke in a form agreed upon, and in a foreign language:

"N'est ce pas?"

"Maman, it is time to dine, n'est ce pas?"

"Maman, we ought to go to the cinema show to-night, n'est ce pas?"

However, after much thought, Strevenko devised a plan for unearthing secret plots. He washed his hair with peroxide of hydrogen, shaved himself where necessary, and became a fairhaired individual of gloomy appearance. Then he put on a sad-coloured suit so that no one could recognise him.

At night he went out into the street, and walked about as if deep in thought. Noticing a citizen stealing along, he pounced upon him from the left and whispered in a provocative manner:

"Comrade, are you really satisfied with your existence?"

The citizen slackened his pace, as if considering the question; but as soon as a policeman appeared in the distance he shouted in accordance with his invariable practice:

"Policeman, hold him."

Strevenko sprang over the fence like a tiger, and as he sat in the stinging nettles thought to himself:

"You cannot get hold of them like this; they act in a perfectly legal manner, the devils."

In the meantime the money allowed him was disappearing. He put on a less dismal-looking suit, and tried another way of trapping people. Boldly approaching a citizen he would ask him:

"Would you like to become an agent-provocateur, sir?"

And the citizen would reply coolly:

"What is the salary?"

Others declined politely:

"No, thank you, I am already engaged."

"Well," thought Oronty, "how am I to catch them?"

In the meantime the money allowed him was gradually melting away.

In the course of his search he looked in at the headquarters of the Society for the Many-Sided Use of Empty Egg-Shells, but discovered that the society enjoys the exalted patronage of three bishops, and of a general of gendarmerie; that it meets once a year and gets a special permit each time from St Petersburg. Oronty still failed to catch plotters and the money allowed him seemed to him to have galloping consumption.

Oronty was thoroughly annoyed:

"I'll soon show them!"

And he began to act quite openly. He would go up to a citizen and ask him straight out:

"Are you satisfied with your existence?"

"Quite satisfied."

"Well, but the authorities are dissatisfied. Please come along."

And if anyone said that he was not satisfied, the result was, of course, the same:

"Take him along!" said Strevenko.

"But, excuse me."

"What?"

"But I am dissatisfied because their measures are not sufficiently rigorous."

"Indeed? Take him."

Thus, in the course of three weeks, he had gathered together ten thousand men and women of one sort and another. At first he imprisoned them where he could; then he began to hang them; but for the sake of economy he did it at the expense of the citizens themselves.

Everything went very well till, one day, a superior official, who chanced to be out beagling in the outskirts of the town, saw unusual animation in the fields; a picture of the peaceful activity of citizens presented itself to him. They were reviling one another, hanging and burying one another, whilst Strevenko walked amongst them staff in hand, barking out words of encouragement:

"Hurry up, you melancholy owl, and be more cheerful about it! And you reverend-looking old man, there, why do you look so stupefied? The noose is ready; get into it; don't keep the others waiting. Whoa, lad; why do you get into the noose before your father? Gentlemen, don't be in such a hurry; your turn will come right enough. You have been patient for years, awaiting pacification by the Government; you can afford to wait a few minutes. You, peasant, where are you going? You ignoramus!"

The superior official, mounted on a handsome horse, looked on and thought:

"Anyway, he has got hold of a good many. He is a fine fellow! That is why all the windows in the town are boarded up."

But suddenly, to his utter astonishment, he saw his own aunt hanging by the neck, her feet dangling above the ground:

"Who gave the order?"

Strevenko was on the spot and said:

"I, your Excellency."

"Well, brother, you are a fool. You are simply wasting money belonging to the Treasury. Let me see your account."

Strevenko produced his account, wherein it was stated:

"In execution of the order concerning the extermination of those who have opinions of their own I have unearthed and imprisoned 10,107 persons of both sexes. Of this number:

"729 persons of both sexes have been killed; 541 persons of both sexes have been hanged; 937 persons of both sexes have been crippled for life; 317 persons of both sexes have died prematurely; 63 persons of both sexes have committed suicide; total number exterminated, 1876.

"Total Cost: Roubles 16,884—i.e. at the rate of 7 roubles per person.

"Deficit: Roubles 884."

The superior official, was staggered. He muttered in a fury:

"A deficit! You Fuegian! The whole of your Terra Del Fuego, together with the king and you yourself, is not worth eight hundred roubles. Just think of it! If you are going to steal money like that what am I to do?—I, who occupy a rank ten times higher? If we have such appetites Russia won't last us three years. There are many others besides you who want to live. Can't you understand that? And besides, you have wrongly included three hundred and eighty persons, for three hundred and seventeen 'died prematurely' and sixty-three committed suicide. You swindler, you have included them as well."

"Your Excellency," Oronty tried to justify himself, "but I drove them into such a state of mind that they loathed their life."

"And seven roubles a head for that? Besides, no doubt a lot of those included were not concerned in the matter at all. The total population of the town is only twelve thousand. No, my friend, I will bring you before the court."

A very strict investigation was accordingly made into the activity of the Fuegian, and he was found guilty of having misappropriated nine hundred and sixteen roubles belonging to the Treasury.

The court that tried Oronty was a just one; he was sentenced to three months' imprisonment, and his career was spoilt. The Fuegian was out of sight for three months.

It is no easy matter to please the authorities.

PASSIVE RESISTANCE

A kind-hearted man debated what was best to do and finally decided:

"I will cease to resist evil by violence. I will overcome it by patience."

This man was not of a weak character. Having decided, he waited patiently.

Igemon's assistants, hearing of this, reported:

"Amongst the citizens who are under supervision there is one who has suddenly begun to conduct himself in a strange manner. He does not move about or say anything: evidently he is trying to deceive the authorities, pretending not to exist at all."

Igemon flew into a rage:

"How, who does not exist? Bring him into my presence."

The citizen was brought and Igemon commanded: "Search him."

They searched him, deprived him of everything about him that was of value, such as his watch and gold wedding ring.

They scraped the fillings out of his teeth, for they were gold. They took off his new braces, cut off his buttons and reported:

"Ready, Igemon."

"Well, anything found?"

"Nothing but what was superfluous about him; we have rid him of it all."

"And in his head?"

"There seems to be nothing in his head."

"Let him in."

The citizen came into Igemon's presence, and from the way he held up his trousers Igemon saw and understood his complete readiness for all kinds of contingencies in life. But Igemon desired to make an impression upon him which would crush his soul, so he roared ferociously:

"Oh, citizen, you have come!"

And the citizen admitted quietly:

"Yes, I have brought the whole of me."

"What is it you are doing?"

"I, Igemon, am doing nothing, I have simply decided to conquer by patience." Igemon bristled with anger and roared: "Again? To conquer again?"

"Yes, to overcome evil."

"Be silent!"

"I did not mean you."

Igemon did not believe him and said:

"If not me then whom do you mean?"

"Myself."

Igemon was surprised.

"Wait a minute. What evil do you mean?"

"Resistance."

"You are lying."

"Heaven knows I am not."

Igemon broke into a perspiration.

"What is the matter with him?" he thought, looking at the man; and, after pondering for some moments, he asked him:

"What is it you want?"

"I don't want anything."

"Really nothing at all?"

"Nothing. Merely permit me to teach the people patience by my own example." Igemon pondered again, biting his moustache. He was possessed of a soul which took delight in daydreams. He liked to steam himself in a Turkish bath, giving forth voluptuous sounds of pleasure. Generally speaking, he was in favour of enjoying the pleasures of life. There was only one thing he could not stand, and that was rudeness and opposition, against which he acted in a manner that rendered everything soft, reducing to a pulp the bones and gristle of the resisters. But when not busy enjoying life or crushing citizens he liked to indulge in daydreams about universal peace, and in the salvation of the soul.

He looked with embarrassment at the citizen and said:

"Not long since you thought the reverse, and now?"

Then, overcome by more tender feelings, he asked with a sigh: "How did it come about?"

The citizen replied:

"Evolution."

"Well, brother, such is our life. First it is one thing, then another. There is failure in everything. We sway from side to side, but we do not know on which side to lie down, we cannot choose."

And Igemon sighed again, for he knew that the man loved the fatherland which had nurtured him. All kinds of dangerous thoughts were running through Igemon's head:

"True, it is pleasant to see a citizen yielding and peaceful. But if everybody ceased to resist, would it not cut off our daily allowance and our travelling expenses? We might lose our bonuses too.... No, it cannot be that there is no resistance left in him. The rogue is pretending; he must be put to the test. To what use shall I put him? Make of him an agent-provocateur? The expression of his face is indefinite, his lack of personality could not be hidden by any mask. Besides, his powers of oratory are evidently not great. Make him a hangman? He has not strength enough."

At last a thought struck him and he said to his subordinates:

"Put this happy man in the third section of the fire brigade to clean the stables."

It was done. The citizen strenuously cleaned the stables without saying a word, while Igemon looked on, touched by his patience; his confidence in the man was steadily increasing.

"But if everybody behaved like that?"

After a short trial he promoted him into his own office and asked him to copy a false report which he himself had written about the income and expenditure of various sums. The citizen copied it and kept silence.

Igemon was touched to such an extent that he shed tears.

"No, he is a useful man, although literate."

He called the citizen to him and said:

"I believe in you! Go and preach your truth, but keep your eyes open."

The citizen went to market-places, to fairs, through large towns, through small towns, saying everywhere:

"What are you doing?"

The people saw that he was unusually meek and this, together with his personality, caused them to confide in him. They confessed to him all of which they were guilty, and even revealed to him their inmost thoughts. One of them wanted to steal something and to evade being punished for it, another wanted to cheat somebody, a third simply wanted to slander somebody. All of them, like genuine Russians, wanted to get out of having any duties in life, and to forget all their obligations.

He said to them:

"Oh, give up all this, because it is said: 'All existence is suffering, but it becomes suffering through desire; hence, in order to destroy suffering, you must destroy desire.' Let us cease to desire and all evil will disappear of its own accord; truly it will."

The people, of course, were glad. It seemed reasonable and was very simple. Where they happened to stand they lay down. They all felt relieved.

After what interval is not recorded, but there came a time when Igemon noticed that all was peace around him, and he was struck by fear. Still he tried to put on a brave face:

"The rogues are pretending."

Meanwhile, the insects, continuing to fulfil their natural obligations, were beginning to multiply in an unnatural way, and becoming more and more arrogant in their actions.

"What silence," thought Igemon, wriggling and scratching himself all over.

He called a willing citizen to him:

"Come, free me from the superfluous."

He answered:

"I cannot."

"What?"

"I cannot, because even if they do annoy you, they are living things, and——"

"I will make a corpse of you this minute."

"As you will."

And so in everything; they all answered him with one voice:

"As you will."

But as soon as he asked them to fulfil his will he found it a most tedious task. Igemon's palace was falling to pieces; it was overrun with rats, which ate up the deeds, and died of the resultant poisoning. Igemon himself was sinking deeper and deeper into inaction. He lay on the sofa daydreaming about the past. How good life was in those days! The inhabitants tried to resist his orders in all kinds of ways. Some of them had to be executed, which meant obituary feasts with pancakes and free drinks. Or a citizen would embark upon some new enterprise; it was necessary to go and stop him, which meant travelling expenses. When he reported to the proper quarter that in the district entrusted to him all the inhabitants had been exterminated he used to receive a special bonus and a fresh batch was sent into the district.

Igemon was daydreaming about the past, but his neighbours, the Igemons of other tribes, lived as they had lived before, on the old basis. The inhabitants opposed them on every occasion, and as vigorously as they could. All was noise and disorder. The Igemons rushed hither and thither, without any special object. They found it profitable and, in a general way, interesting.

And the thought struck Igemon:

"By Jove! the citizen has fooled me."

He jumped up, rushed through the whole district, shaking people, pummelling them, and shouting:

"Get up! Wake up! Arise!"

It was no good. He seized them by their collars, but the collars were rotten and broke away.

"The devils," shouted Igemon, greatly agitated. "What are you doing? Look at your neighbours—even China——"

The inhabitants were silent as they clung to the soil.

"O Lord!" said Igemon in disgust, "what is to be done?"

And he resorted to deception; he bent over an inhabitant and whispered into his ear:

"Oh, citizen, the fatherland is in danger. It is, I swear. By all that's holy! it is in great danger. Get up; it is necessary to resist. They say that all kinds of activities will be allowed. Citizen!" But the dying citizen only murmured: "My fatherland is in God."

The others were simply silent, like offended corpses.

"The cursed fatalists!" shouted Igemon in despair. "Get up! All kinds of resistance is allowed."

One who had been a jolly fellow, and had distinguished himself by knocking out people's teeth, raised himself a little, looked round and said:

"What shall we resist? There is nothing to resist."

"But the vermin?"

"We are used to it."

Igemon's reason received the last shock. He got up and roared in awe-inspiring tones:

"I permit you everything, fellows; save yourselves; do what you like; everything is permitted—eat each other."

The calm and quiet were delightful! Igemon saw that all was over.

He started to cry aloud; hot tears ran down his cheeks; he tore his hair and roared, calling upon them:

"Citizens, dear fellows, what am I to do? Must I make a revolution myself? Bethink yourselves; it is historically necessary; it is nationally inevitable. You see that it is impossible for me alone to make a revolution. I have not even police for that, the vermin have eaten them."

The citizens only blinked their eyes; even if they had been pierced by a stake they would not have uttered a sound.

So they all died in silence, and Igemon, in utter despair, last of all.

From this it follows that even in patience we must observe a certain amount of moderation.

MAKING A SUPERMAN

The wisest of the citizens pondered the following problem:—

"What does it mean? Wherever one looks everything is at sixes and sevens."

And after much thought they concluded:

"It is because we have no personality. It is necessary for us to create a central thinking organ which shall be quite free from any sort of bias, which shall be capable of raising itself above everything, which shall stand out from everything and everybody—in the same way as a goat from amongst a flock of sheep." Somebody said:

"Brothers, have we not already suffered enough from central personalities?" They did not like this.

"That seems to savour of politics, and even of civic sorrow."

Somebody insisted:

"But how can we ignore politics if politics penetrate everything? The facts are that the prisons are overcrowded, that in the hard labour prisons it is impossible to turn round; and to remedy this we must enlarge the scope of our rights."

But they answered him sternly:

"This, sir, is idealism, and it is time you left it alone. A new man is wanted, and nothing else."

After this they set to work to create a man according to the methods referred to in the traditions of the holy fathers: they spat on the ground, and began to mix the spittle with earth. Then they smeared themselves up to the ears with the mixture, but the results were poor. In their eagerness they trampled rare flowers into the ground, and destroyed useful cereals. They tried hard, they sweated in the earnestness of their efforts; but there was no result—nothing but a waste of words and mutual accusations of creative incapacity. They even put the elements out of patience by their zeal: whirlwinds began to blow, the heat became intense, it thundered, and the rain poured down in torrents; the ground became sodden, and the whole atmosphere saturated with heavy odours, so that it was difficult to breathe.

However, from time to time this wrestling with the elements seemed to come to an end, and a new personality came into God's world.

There was general rejoicing everywhere, but it was short-lived, and soon turned into oppressive embarrassment. For, if a new personality arose out of the peasant soil, it became forthwith a polished merchant, and, starting business at once, began to sell the fatherland piecemeal to foreigners—first of all at forty-five copecks[6] a plot, and afterwards going to such lengths that it wanted to sell a whole district, with all its live stock and thinking machines.

If they stirred up a new man on merchant soil he either was born a degenerate or at once became a bureaucrat. If they did it on a nobleman's estate, beings arose, as they had done before, who seemed intent upon swallowing up the whole revenue of the state. On the soil of the middle class and petty property-owners all sorts of wild thistles grew: agents-provocateurs, Nihilists, pacifists, and goodness knows what.

"But we already have all these in a sufficient quantity," the wise citizens confessed to each other.

And they were sadly puzzled.

"We have made some kind of mistake in the technique of creation," they said.

"But what was the mistake?"

---

[6] Elevenpence.—Trans.

They sat in the mud and thought very hard.

Then they began to upbraid one another:

"You, Selderey Lavrovich, you spit too much, and in all directions."

"And you, Kornishon Lukich, are too faint-hearted to do likewise."

The newly born Nihilists, pretending to be Vaska Buslayeffs, looked at everything with contempt and shouted:

"Oh, you vegetables, try and think what place is best, and we will help you to spit on it."

And they spat and spat.

They all seemed bored and irritable with one another; and they were covered with mud.

Just at that time Mitya Korofyshkin, nicknamed "Steel Claw," who was playing truant from school, passed by. He was a pupil in the second class of the Miamlin Gymnasium, and was known as a collector of foreign stamps. As he passed he saw the people sitting in a puddle and spitting, deep in thought.

"Grown-ups, and they bespatter themselves like that!" thought Mitya contemptuously; which was natural in one of his tender years.

He peeped to see if there was not a teacher in their midst, and not noticing one he inquired:

"What are you doing in the puddle, uncles?"

One of the citizens, resenting the question, immediately began to argue:

"Where do you see a puddle? It is simply a reflection of the primordial chaos."

"And what are you doing?"

"We are trying to create a new man. We are sick of people like you."

Mitya became interested.

"After whose likeness?"

"What do you mean? We want to create somebody unlike anyone else. Go away."

As Mitya was a child, and not yet versed in the secrets of nature, he, of course, was glad of the opportunity to be present at such an important affair, and he asked them simply:

"Will you make him with three legs?"

"What are you saying?"

"How funnily he will run!"

"Go away, boy."

"Or with wings! What a fine thing it would be! Make him with wings, by Jove! and let him kidnap teachers, like the condor did in 'The Children of Captain Grant.' There, of course, the condor does not kidnap a teacher, but it would be better if he did kidnap the teacher."

"Boy, you are talking nonsense, and it is sinful nonsense. Remember your prayers before and after your lessons."

But Mitya was a boy with a fertile imagination, and he became very excited.

"As the teacher is going to the gymnasium it will grab him by the collar and carry him away to somewhere in the air, it makes no difference where. The teacher will simply kick and drop all his books—I hope the books will never be found."

"Boy, have reverence for your elders."

"And the teacher shouts to his wife from above: 'Good-bye, I am going to heaven like Elijah and Enoch,' And his wife kneels in the middle of the road and whimpers: 'My school teacher! Oh, my school teacher!'"

They got quite angry with him.

"Get away, you are jabbering nonsense. There are many who can do that. You are beginning too soon."

They drove him away, but he stopped before he had gone far, thought a while, and asked:

"Do you really mean it?"

"Of course."

"And it won't work?"

They sighed sullenly and said:

"No; leave us alone."

Then Mitya moved a little farther away, put out his tongue and mocked them:

"I know why! I know why!"

He ran away, but they chased him, and as they were used to changing the scene of their operations and running from place to place they soon caught him. Then they began to beat him.

"Oh, you scamp ... cheeking your elders."

Mitya cried and implored:

"Uncles, I will give you a Soudanese stamp—I have a duplicate.... I will make you a present of my penknife——"

But they tried to frighten him with the headmaster's name.

"Uncles, really and truly, I will never tease you again. Now I have really guessed why a new man cannot be created."

"Speak!"

"Don't hold me so tight!"

They released him all but his hands, and he said to them:

"Uncles, it is not the proper soil. The soil is no good, on my word of honour. You may spit as much as you like, nothing will come of it. For, when God created Adam in his image, the land belonged to nobody. Now it all belongs to someone or other; therefore man now belongs to somebody. Spitting makes no difference whatever."

They were so dumbfounded that they dropped their hands; Mitya rushed away from them, and making a trumpet of his hands shouted:

"You red-skinned Comanches! Iroquois!"

But they all went back to the puddle, and the wisest of them said:

"Colleagues, let us resume our occupation. Let us forget this boy, for he is very likely a socialist in disguise."

Oh, Mitya, Mitya!